AVERNUS ISLAND

THE MONSTERS & MAYHEM COLLECTION
BOOK TWO

PATRICK MCNULTY

THE MINISTRY OF MONSTERS PRESS

To my family who have sat patiently, and listened to me say, "What do you think about this?" before I launch into a new crazy pitch for a story. Thanks for listening and helping me sift through the coal for the diamonds.

ONE

OAK BAY, OREGON

Ruth Coolidge had finally stopped screaming.

Frustrated and exhausted she stomped out of her own bedroom, chasing the echoes of her last words into the narrow hall, and promptly collapsed to the dusty floorboards a whimpering, shuddering mess.

And that's where she sat, minutes later. An old woman crumpled on the floor, her pale legs wrapped in compression stockings tucked demurely beneath her, the mud brown house dress decorated with tiny, faded flowers puddled around her thin frame.

The thunder in her chest was spent. The sharp, hurtful words had all been said. Knives thrown across the divide between them that left wounds on both sides.

Ruth felt hollowed out. Gutted, as she sat there as tears spilled down her face. She picked absently at the hem of her dress and thought of how she could have done things differently.

How she could have told Marcus in a different way, a gentler way. A way that didn't end with her screaming herself hoarse. She imagined a scenario where his dark eyes didn't flash with so much pain and hurt, and worst of all, betrayal. She had waited until the last possible second, but still, it was too soon.

Ruth had no idea.

She had assumed that the secret buried was too well hidden. Too deep in the earth to ever see the light of day. But she was wrong. So wrong. She could wait no longer.

She had cooked him his favorite meal; breakfast for dinner, complete with fluffy buttermilk pancakes and plump breakfast sausages, fried eggs, and deep fried home fries.

He had been suspicious as she cooked this spur of the moment feast. He wasn't a stupid man. She saw him watching her from his seat at the kitchen table, over the edge of the Oak Bay Gazette, one shaggy eyebrow raised.

The meal was perfect, if she could be so bold, and as he sipped his after-dinner coffee and before the one cigarette he allowed himself after dinner, she sat across from him at the kitchen table. Hands folded, she felt the ball of ice rolling in her stomach growing bigger with every passing second.

"You all right?" Marcus asked, when the silence spread out too thin. She knew he could feel it. She felt it too. Like a presence, an energy, that started small but had bloomed. Spreading out, filling the space. Her chest felt heavy, and she struggled to breathe.

He knew something was bothering her. You didn't live with someone for decades without learning their particular tells.

"Fine." Ruth had answered, with a flicker of a smile, looking anything but fine. Looking about as relaxed as if she were sitting on a land mine.

"*Ruth*." Marcus had said, looking at her now. "You've been acting shifty all day."

"Have not." She said, giving his arm a playful slap.

He didn't say another word. He didn't have to. He slipped his gnarled hand over hers and waited. He wasn't always so patient, but he had worked at it. Experience had taught him he couldn't force her to talk. He couldn't force her to do anything she didn't want to. And she desperately didn't want to do what she was about to do.

And even then, even with no time left to stall, she thought of lying. Of telling him she felt poorly. Maybe a touch of the stomach flu that had swept through their little village. Talk about how Margaret Bleeker and one deputy down at the police station got the trots so bad they got a prescription from Doc Baker for Pedialyte.

A false narrative came to her so formed she actually thought about using it. But she couldn't. Not now. It was too late. It had been too late for a while now, if she were honest with herself.

At night she would lie awake when the lights were out, and she would listen to the wind that swept over the Pacific. Hear it scream onto the mainland and shake their little clapboard house. She could hear it then. She swore she could.

The soft sounds of fingers digging through soil. Getting louder and louder, as the secret clawed through the rocky land of the island, desperate for the light.

"I have to tell you something." She whispered and felt her breath being squeezed from her lungs. She could feel Marcus' dark eyes on her like hands closing around her throat.

"Something, I never wanted to tell you...but it can't wait anymore."

IT WAS cold on the floor.

As the sun fell and the wind picked up its nimble fingers found a way around the frame of the tiny round window at the end of the hall.

The cool Pacific breeze moved over her with gentle fingers, slipping through the strands of gray hair that had come loose from her ponytail and cooled the tears left to dry on her cheeks.

She swiped at her face and finger combed the stray tangles of hair, as she scraped them back in line.

Ruth shifted her weight and broke the rust that had already begun to form over her ancient joints. A bright flare of pain shot through her right hip, the result of allowing that sharp curve of bone to press into the cold floorboards for too long. A hiss bled through her clenched teeth as she slowly climbed to all fours, and then, using the wall for support, struggled to her feet.

Marcus was still in her bedroom. She hadn't heard him move after his bulk dropped onto the edge of the bed. The springs rusted from decades of ocean air squeaked and groaned as the old mattress bore his weight.

Slowly, she crept down the hallway, her trained footsteps avoiding the spots on the floorboards that hid the creaks.

Her wrinkled hand found the doorframe and she peeked into the only bedroom she had ever known.

Marcus Avernus sat like a sphinx perched on the edge of her bed. He wore the ratty gray cardigan, the color of storm clouds, she had knitted for him years ago. She remembered that she had given it to him on his forty-seventh birthday, and it had almost immediately unravelled and fallen apart.

Since she had offered to knit him a new one, her skills had greatly improved. But he had adamantly refused, allowing her only to mend the current sweater, and nothing more.

Now, Marcus' broad shoulders slumped forward. His long arms ended at gnarled, arthritic hands that resembled knotted roots. In those hands, clasped between his thick fingers, was a small, leather-bound diary.

It wasn't Ruth's diary, but it had been her responsibility. Her burden to keep all these years since her mother died and left her here.

Left her alone.

The last of the watery sunlight fell through the only

window in her bedroom: a small rectangle no bigger than a porthole that overlooked the ocean beyond.

Tiny motes of dust spun lazily in the shaft of light without a care in the world. Ruth envied them.

She could tell by the tilt of his head that his dark brown eyes were fixed on something out at sea.

She didn't have to ask. She knew what he was staring at.

A small spit of land a few football fields square, less than three miles off the coast. A rocky, desolate place avoided by the locals and only visited by curious teenagers, and usually only once.

Avernus Island.

His family's island.

Marcus' island.

Ruth edged around the doorway, gripping the chipped woodwork, as she eased her way across the threshold.

"Marcus?"

Ruth's voice was small and barely above a whisper, but Marcus flinched as if he were lashed. He blinked and drew a wheezing breath.

"Marcus, please." She said, and dared to move closer to him. She wished he would just look at her. If he did he would see it wasn't her fault. She didn't do this. She only told him to protect him. To keep him safe.

"Talk to me." She begged.

Marcus rose without a word from the bed, the rusted springs rejoicing as he did, and dropped the thin diary on the flowered coverlet.

He turned toward the door and the woman standing in his way, and for a moment their eyes met. His were ringed black and bloodshot, but they were clear. In a glance she knew better than to try and stop him. To even try and reason with him now.

He stomped toward the door in a straight line and Ruth scurried out of his path, only to follow him like a loyal soldier, as he thundered his way down to the main level of the house.

She stood by and watched as Marcus lifted his heavy raincoat from the peg by the door and slipped his arms into the sleeves.

"Marcus, *enough*." She said, as she slipped behind him and blocked the front door, her arms crossed over her thin chest.

"Move, Ruth." He told her, his voice more of a growl. *"Now."*

"Where are you going?"

He answered her with a look that bore into her.

"You can't go now." She said.

"You want to go out and see for yourself do it tomorrow. It's too late now. It'll be dark soon."

He shifted in place, and his eyes flicked to the darkening windows as the waning twilight bled away.

"You know it can't wait." He told her.

"It's waited this long, it can wait another day."

"Do you have any idea what this means? If this is true? What this will do?" He said, as he inched toward her. His breath reeked of coffee and nicotine.

"I have responsibilities, Ruth. People depend on me. Contracts have been signed."

"Marcus, you have to believe me, that I did this...that I told you, because I...I didn't want to hurt you. Please. Please, believe me."

Ruth could feel her resolve crumble. She could feel her whole body as it trembled and shook, as she waited for Marcus to speak. To believe her. She never wanted to hurt him, but the secret she kept, was forced to keep, was a voracious cancer that ate more of her every day.

"Please, don't go." She said. "Wait til morning. *Please.*"

She reached for him then and he didn't flinch. Didn't pull away. The thin fingers of Ruth's right hand cupped Marcus' warm cheek through his short gray beard, and he leaned into her touch. His hand slid over hers and squeezed. Marcus' gaze softened, but it didn't change his mind.

"This can't wait." He told her. "Not anymore. You know that."

Marcus kissed her fingertips and then, without another word, slipped around Ruth to the front door, and into the growing darkness.

The garden shed stank of gasoline, motor oil, and the cloying scent of old grass clippings.

Marcus moved inside, careful not to trip on a rake left in his path, and reached up in the dark, his body moving with muscle memory, to grasp the thin chain. With a sharp tug the single bare bulb mounted in the ceiling spread warm light over the cramped little space.

A waist-high counter, scarred and stained by a lifetime of home improvement projects, crafting ideas, and school assignments ran along the left side of the shed.

Atop stood a neat row of mason jars loaded with screws, nails, bolts, and washers. At the far end, a powerful halogen flashlight and the battery packs belonging to his power tools sat quietly charging. Small LED lights, green across the board.

An ancient lawnmower sat waiting for summer against the back wall, while the right side of the shed was occupied by tall red tool chests, the kind with sliding drawers. The wall itself, was dominated by a peg board where the larger tools of his collection waited patiently to be used.

Marcus shuffled to the end of the counter and unplugged the flashlight from its cradle and switched it on. The powerful halogen beam shot a laser of harsh white light at the back wall and banished the shadows to the deepest corners of the tiny garage. Satisfied, he turned off the light and stuffed it into a canvas bag he had slung over his shoulder.

Next, he stood at the pegboard and pulled down the tools he needed: a sixteen-pound sledgehammer, a smaller, four-pound hammer, and a four-foot steel crowbar.

From the tall tool chest, he found the drawer with his plastic work goggles and slipped those into the bag as well. That was all he needed, he thought, to come back blinded in one eye.

Marcus didn't know what would be worse, the blindness or hearing Ruth tell him, *How many times have I told you to wear those goddamn safety glasses?*

He stuffed the tools into the canvas carry-all and killed the light.

OUTSIDE, the razored wind had strengthened in the last few minutes, and he could see a few whitecaps rolling in from the dark water.

He pulled down his knit cap to protect his ears, always the first part of his body to get cold and ache, ever since he got frostbite so bad as a kid, while ice fishing with his father, he nearly lost his hearing.

Ten steps down the gravel driveway, his boots crunched toward the dock. The bag of tools bounced against his hip, the strap dug a painful groove into his shoulder, and he realized that Ruth had been right. This was a fool's errand, and the daylight was all but gone. By the time he got to the island it would be full dark.

It didn't matter.

This couldn't wait.

There was no time.

He shifted the strap of the canvas bag to a slightly less painful position and kept his feet moving.

Without having to look over his shoulder, he knew Ruth would stand on the back porch with one of his heavy winter coats wrapped around her skinny frame, as she watched him go.

Marcus left the gravel driveway and stomped onto the pier that jutted over a small bit of beach at the end of their property, as a blast of icy wind roared off the sea. It knifed through his clothes and cut into the exposed flesh of his face, as the old boards thumped and shook under his weight.

He made his way to his small fishing boat that bobbed and swayed in the dark water, as it pulled on its moorings, angling toward the open sea as if it wanted to go out.

Marcus dropped the bag of tools, into the bottom of

the boat, glad to be rid of the weight, and massaged his aching shoulder. He took his seat at the rear and withdrew the battery-powered lantern.

Marcus peered through the gloom as twilight quickly bled away to full dark, and saw the old island staring back.

Waiting.

His mind flashed to the diary and the words written there in a spidery black script. The secret hidden for generations.

It couldn't be true.

He shook his head, clearing the thought from his mind and turned his attention to the motor.

It's not true.

It had been a while since he had taken the boat out, but after he goosed the engine with some gas, the boat's tiny motor started on the third pull.

Marcus removed the mooring ropes from the cleats and pushed away from the dock. He slipped leather gloves over his aching hands and pulled up the collar of his raincoat. This would not be a pleasant cruise. He was already freezing and the ten minute ride out to the island would not improve that.

Marcus eased the throttle up. The engine coughed and whined as it powered the little boat through the dark water and toward the shadowed strip of land that is Avernus Island.

The trip across the reach, as the locals called it, was longer than Marcus expected. With his head down and buried into his chest, he kept one eye on the west side of the island where he wanted to land, and one hand on the throttle.

The wind howled and screamed like a wild animal as it bounced his little skiff across a seemingly endless parade of angry looking waves. Freezing spray splashed over him, and covered him in a thin skin of ice.

Marcus was forced to slow down as he made landfall in the dark praying the tiny aluminum boat didn't strike one of the sharp rocks that lined the coast, ripping a hole in the hull and forcing him to camp on the island overnight.

Luckily, he knew the island better than anyone and soon navigated the tiny craft into a safe harbor. A stretch of beach protected on either side by a pair of towering boulders. The massive rocks had erupted from the sandy soil thousands of years ago, and were sharpened over time by the wind and snow and rain. They were angled toward the sea as if to repel intruders, or offer a warning to would-be visitors.

Marcus gunned the little engine and drove the boat up onto the sandy shore as far as he could go, and then killed the power. He climbed over the side and dragged the boat up onto the beach, out of the ocean's reach. He looped a rope from the bow to the trunk of a withered tree and secured the knot.

Next, he dragged the canvas bag from the boat and withdrew the flashlight and snapped it on.

He slung the bag over his shoulder and, with a last look to the boat and the twinkling lights of the mainland beyond, he headed for the barracks.

THREE

Trees didn't grow on the island, as much as they clawed through the rocky earth in search of the sun. The end result was gray, withered trunks the color of bone, that were twisted by the wind and rain, and warped into winding shapes by the crushing weight of snow and ice. What branches remained were the skeletal fingers of frozen witches, reaching for the sun.

But the haunted, spectral trees were all but hidden by a forest of stone.

Millions of years ago, hundreds and thousands of jagged rocks had burst through the coarse ground in the sharpened angles of broken swords. Some as large as school buses, others as small as children, which created a granite maze, essentially fencing off and protecting the center of the island from the coast.

This was one reason the US Army had leased the property from Marcus' father to build a temporary barracks during the Second World War.

Hundreds of soldiers were housed on the property and trained to kill and maim, and when the war ended so did the Army's lease.

Marcus picked his way through the maze of stone, his powerful flashlight chasing away shadows and creating new ones that scurried away from his light as he shuffled over the coarse sand.

It didn't take long if you knew where you were going, and Marcus knew this island intimately. As a boy he had explored every inch. Fishing off its coasts, collecting shells from its beaches and even diving from the larger rocks that overhung the deep water.

By his fifteenth birthday he had explored every room of the crumbling barracks, even though he swore to his parents, up and down, he would never do something so reckless.

During a late night bonfire right here on the rocky shore, he had his first kiss. A soft brushing of the lips with a shy, but cute freshman, Rita McMillan.

He stood for a second in the dark, as the surf pounded the beach behind him, the memory of that first kiss so fresh in his mind. He remembered the kiss tasted like peaches.

The wind howled, its voice rising and falling as it swept through the labyrinth of rocks and shook Marcus from his reverie. He blinked and shook his head.

Another senior moment. He thought.

And they were getting worse. The once steel trap of his memory was being eaten by the rust of old age.

Allowing more and more of his memories to slip through the cracks, and into the darkness.

They began as little gaps. Blank spots where he would arrive at the kitchen counter and not realize what he was doing there, or he would stand in front of a cabinet and not remember how he got there.

Ruth laughed off these episodes as the cost of getting old and Marcus did his best to dismiss them too, as he played along. But they *were* getting worse. The blank spots. The dark areas were getting longer and longer. He wondered how soon before his world, his entire life, would cross over into that dark place.

His feet were freezing, and he could barely feel his toes wriggling in his boots. He needed to do this and get back before he froze solid and became another stone in the forest.

Marcus pushed on, head down. His breath steamed out in the ragged puffs of a tired locomotive as he made his way, turning left and right through the towering maze. The sun slipped completely beyond the horizon and shadows flooded in.

At the end of the winding maze, Marcus stepped through a natural arch created by two massive boulders that had punched through the ground eons ago and welded themselves together ten feet above his head.

Beyond the arch lay a wide circular courtyard that had been manually cleared by the Army before construction could begin on the barracks beyond.

Using explosives and heavy machinery the Army engineers had created a blank slate in the center of the island.

The one peculiar item they didn't destroy, the one feature they were forbidden to touch, was an ancient stone well. The well became the central feature, the only feature, of a courtyard sanitized of every struggling tree and jagged rock in a five acre square area.

Marcus swept the beam of his halogen light across the courtyard. The hard ground bore the dark circular wounds of old campfires. Crushed beer cans that dotted the landscape winked and sparked in the bright light. Plastic bags and the rags of discarded clothes fluttered in the harsh wind, caught in the grasp of thin, but hardy weeds that had graduated and matured into dense brush and fledgling trees.

Thunder grumbled somewhere in the near distance, followed by a flash of lightning.

A storm was coming.

He would be soaked to the bone riding back to mainland. Marcus eyed the sky to decipher its intentions as thunder rumbled again. A low growl he could feel in his chest. Closer this time, and his suspicions were confirmed.

He shook his head thinking about the *I told you so,* that was bound to come from Ruth when he got home.

Marcus swore under his breath and hurried to the well at the center of the courtyard. The well was larger than its mainland counterparts, and was easily five feet across.

Its walls rose four feet from ground level, and were comprised entirely of black volcanic rock. It was a marvel to behold, and he knew that although, technically the island was private property, tourists came to visit the island every summer just to see it.

The wide shaft was criss-crossed in a thorny gray vine that looked prepared to guard the well from any invaders who dared to draw too close. Still, even with the vine draped across it and the dust and grime that collected on its exterior, the wall of the well sparkled like a giant dark jewel in the beam of his flashlight.

A crude capstone adorned the top of the well for as long as Marcus could remember. It was hastily constructed and some of the concrete used had dripped down the glossy black sides to dry in rough smears and jagged lumps.

His father, years ago, before Alzheimer's erased the man he was and reduced him to a simple child living in a failing, elderly body, had explained that the well had been capped for safety reasons.

The very thought of a useful well in the middle of the ocean was a slightly ridiculous notion. His father explained that he believed that the well wasn't a well at all, but a hydrothermal vent. What it was doing on the island, and not on the bottom of the ocean, his father had no answers.

When pressed about why he didn't allow the Army to clear it away and fill it in, rather than keep the outdated and useless thing, his father was more poetic in his answer. Telling his curious son in a low, raspy voice that had been cured by too many Marlboros, that the well meant something to the Indigenous people who had lived on the island before them. The well marked a special place that was not to be forgotten. A sacred place, that was far more than an obstacle to be cleared away.

He called it the heart of the island.

THE FIRST DIME-SIZED drop of rain fell out of the grumbling sky above and splattered against the capstone.

Marcus manipulated the articulating arms of his flashlight and soon it was transformed into a lantern, which he positioned close to the well.

He examined the capstone and estimated that it was at least four inches thick. Whoever had constructed this had been determined to keep the well sealed. And until today, they had succeeded.

In the indirect light of the lantern, Marcus saw old scars on the rough concrete cap. A history of half-hearted attempts to break through the barrier. Perpetrated by men and women armed with inferior tools, who lacked the necessary energy or proper motivation to complete the task.

They were tourists looking for instant gratification, a quick win, an interesting post for social media. But once the formidable capstone resisted their efforts and the drunken bravado had all been burned away by the output of energy required, they moved on to weaker targets and left the capstone to remain undefeated.

Marcus was not a tourist.

He dropped his canvas bag of tools onto the hard packed ground dotted with rain, and removed the sledgehammer and the safety glasses.

The hammer felt heavier than it did back in the garden shed. As if gravity was stronger here, as it greedily pulled the metal head toward the ground.

Marcus grasped the handle and his leather gloves creaked as he adjusted his grip. The only other sound was the constant whisper of the surf as it crashed against the rocky coast.

Even the storm above had gone quiet. The gentle rainfall had all but stopped, as if the storm held its breath.

As it watched and waited for what came next.

FOUR

Marcus gripped the handle of the sledge and with a grunt, raised it over his head, letting the handle sit in the groove between the cradle of his shoulder and his collarbone.

A gust of wind howled and screamed like a living thing. It shook the brittle walls of the barracks and pushed Marcus off balance.

He found his footing and scanned the dark windows of the derelict building, as his blood pressure climbed into the red.

There was nothing to see. No one was there. The island was dead and always had been since those original inhabitants had left, taking the warmth of their magic with them.

Avernus Island was a desolate place that always felt cold, even in the dead of summer.

Nothing survived here.

Not even birds nested here.

It was one reason locals avoided the place. It was as if the tiny village of Oak Bay had collectively chosen to ignore it. When they gazed out into the Pacific, they looked around it, over it, afraid that something might look back.

No one spoke about the island. Not in private, or in the aisles of the grocery store, or even while wasted on one of the barstools in Sullivan's, the only pub in the tiny village.

Not in whispers.

Never.

But they would talk soon.

Either way. Marcus thought. *They would all talk soon enough.*

Marcus turned his attention back to the covered well and lifted the hammer from his shoulder. He took one last breath and swung the heavy hammer down in a punishing arc, aiming for the center of the capstone.

The sledge hit with a dull gong and a bright flash of pain shot up through his arms in a lightning strike that set fire to his shoulders and exploded across his back.

Marcus staggered and stumbled backward, hurt and disoriented. He dropped the hammer into the dirt and he collapsed onto his ass in a jumble of limbs.

"Sonofabitch!"

Thank God Ruth wasn't here to see that display, he thought. *I would never hear the end of it.*

Marcus struggled to his feet and lifted the hammer from the ground. He set his jaw and gritted his teeth. He took three big steps to the well and brought the hammer down again; this time he was ready for the fallout.

The hammer crashed down on the stone cover with another resounding gong as a brief cloud of dust and bits of stone knifed through the dark.

Marcus dropped the hammer and carried the lantern over to examine the damage. A dime-sized chip of rock was missing from the top, but that was all.

Sonofabitch.

Two strikes in, he was already sweating and a river of ice had formed along his spine, but he shook it off. He had to continue.

Three more blows and Marcus was wheezing. With his hands on his thighs, he shone the light of the lantern across the cover and was rewarded with a hairline crack. Something resembling a smile flickered at the corners of his mouth and he picked up the hammer.

Ten minutes later he was greased with sweat. His shoulders, arms, and back ached and throbbed with a pain that felt as if his upper body had been set on fire from within. His hammer blows had slowed, but he had settled into a rhythm.

Hoist...swing...crash...

Hoist...swing...crash...

With each new strike, clouds of dust peppered with chips of rock, bloomed into the cold, night air.

After a final strike his right hand cramped and he needed to drop the hammer. He massaged the clawed right hand with his left, until he could straighten his fingers.

Next, he tried to move them, wriggling each one until once again, blood began to circulate, and breathed life into the tissues.

Marcus heard the distant sound of running water, a sound he first dismissed as originating from the shore. Or rainwater puddling through the ruin of the barracks. But the sound was closer. Much closer.

He held the lantern up to the capstone and examined the surface. Near the center of the stone, surrounded by the recent battle scars of dents and divots, was a tiny, triangular hole. And water was bubbling up through the gap.

Sweat had dripped on the lenses of the scratched safety goggles and Marcus tossed them aside. He moved the lantern closer, bringing the full power of the beam to bear, and examined the brackish fluid.

The black, viscous liquid gurgled up through the stone in tiny jets and spurts, as if the contents of the well had been under pressure, and he had just provided an escape.

Excited, Marcus leaned closer and dragged the lantern across the stone, casting its glow over the quickly growing puddle that flowed with the viscosity of motor oil.

The stench reached his nose and he yanked his head back. He choked as he tried to spit out the retched taste of rot and disease that had filled his mouth.

He gagged, hands on his thighs as the smell grew, blooming from the hole he had created, and enveloped the well in a dense fog, as if he had broken through a charged sewage line.

What the hell is that?

The smell was making him feel lightheaded. He blinked in the weak light and took a shambling step back toward the well, his gloved hand pressed over his nose and mouth.

The lantern sat where he had left it, atop the capstone. However, the pool of black liquid had swollen. Its glossy black surface had swept past the base of the lantern, and had run to the edge, and beyond, to spill down the sides.

Marcus snatched the lantern and attempted to shake the foul fluid from its base, only to find that it clung to the plastic frame like tar. Smearing and spreading, but not relenting in the slightest.

Careful not to let the disgusting liquid to touch his clothes, or worse yet, his bare flesh, he held the lantern out at arm's length. He stared speechless as the oil continued to bubble and spurt from the tiny aperture he had created.

The stench or rot, and fever and filth emanated from the liquid.

Something was wrong.

Marcus stepped backward step, and then another. He aimed his light at the pool of black liquid and saw that the beam shook in his grasp.

This wasn't happening...what had he done?

The black liquid didn't stop. It bubbled and spurted

out of the capstone and sprayed into the frigid night air like arterial spray.

He watched as the thin rivulets of filth streamed down the sides of the well and followed the curves and hollows of the volcanic glass.

Soon these streams thickened to rivers, as they flowed violently over the side of the well as a black waterfall that reeked of rot, disease, and death.

Marcus held the lantern high, but took a step backward, and then another. He didn't know what he was looking at. He didn't trust his own eyes.

How could this be happening?

The lantern light flickered over the bizarre scene, and for a moment Marcus thought it was a trick. An optical illusion. A clever shadow caused by the movement of the gushing liquid.

He did his best to steady his arm and even took a shuffling step closer to the well.

This couldn't be happening...

The black liquid didn't stop spewing, spurting, jetting into the cold air from the center of the well. With every passing second, it grew more forceful, spraying arterial arcs of black oil to the rhythm of a once cold, still heart, that had just been resurrected from the dead.

Marcus edged closer, the lantern held out at arm's length, its trembling beam illuminating the flooded capstone. The smooth glossy black walls now bathed in a silken ebony veil.

Thunder rolled directly above the island as if angered, and Marcus could feel the deep bass growl in his chest. Lightning clawed at the bruised clouds pregnant with rain, but Marcus was focused on the tips of smooth fingers, glossy with oil, that slowly rose from the dark puddle atop the well's cover.

The greasy hands and thin skeletal arms that impossibly extended skyward until they formed a crowded, circular forest, dripping with gore.

Marcus stood rooted in place. His chest squeezed mercilessly by a fear so intense, so primal, he felt his heart may burst apart as it hammered painfully against the cage of his ribs.

Alarm bells rang in his mind telling him, *begging* him to run. To leave.

NOW.

But he was paralyzed. Powerless to move. Powerless to even look away.

He could barely breathe.

The fingers at the ends of the phantom arms gently curled and flexed, as if testing the air as they probed this new environment.

And then, in one orchestrated movement, the long, delicate fingers and hands reached for the edge of the circular well. They gripped its side, their knuckles blanching white with the effort, as the first soldiers of an unholy legion pulled themselves up out of hell.

Marcus began to scream.

FIVE

NIAGARA FALLS, ONTARIO CANADA

Pete's twenty-four hour diner reeked of old grease and stale coffee, but the place was clean and made a mean meatball sub. Best of all, at this time of night, Dan Avernus had the place all to himself.

He sat at the end of the counter, his back to the narrow hallway leading to the two washrooms, and made sure he had a clear view of the front door. A habit he had developed after being a cop for seventeen years.

Rain tapped at the large windows beyond the cracked red leather booths that lined the low wall. The street outside was deserted, the weather keeping most of the criminal element indoors tonight.

His radio had been busy at the beginning of his shift. A few bar fights, a missing grandmother suffering from dementia, and one bad domestic, where the woman needed stitches over her right eye. But after midnight, it was as if a switch had been flipped and everyone decided to become more reasonable. To calm down and shuffle off to bed. Which was fine by Dan. Just fine.

"Couple more minutes." Pete said, as his narrow, shaved head popped through the little window to the kitchen. "You good, man? You need anything? Coffee?"

Dan shook his head and mustered up a smile that looked more like a grimace and Pete's head disappeared back into the kitchen.

Dan looked down at the counter and saw the playing card between his hands. He frowned. He didn't remember removing it from his wallet, but there it was.

It was a collectible trading card from an online game called *Monster Factory*. A game that his ten-year-old son, Sean, had been obsessed with since it hit the online shelves.

The image on the card was of a wiry teen boy with a knowing grin and a mop of stylish black hair. He was dressed in dark pants and a hooded sweatshirt. Gadgets and gizmos, and glowing magical weapons bulged from his pockets. The bottom edge of the card read: *Milo Jenkins: Monster Hunter.*

I want you to have it.

Dan closed his eyes.

He didn't hear that.

There's no one here but me and Pete. He told himself. *No one.*

Still, he couldn't breathe. He couldn't move, his hands were frozen solid, welded to the counter on either side of the dog-eared trading card.

I want you to have it.

His son's soft, whispered voice curled into his ear as if the boy were actually there, sitting on the next stool, his little feet idly kicking back and forth above the floor.

"You okay, buddy?"

Dan blinked and gasped, not realizing that he had been holding his breath.

Somehow Pete had materialized in front of him, his once white apron splattered with colorful bits of this and that. His prominent Adam's apple continuously bobbed up and down next to a tattoo of a Chinese dragon that curled around the left side of his throat, a permanent reminder of an ill-spent youth.

Pete held a brown paper bag dotted with grease and a can of Coke. A puzzled expression bordering on concern pinched his features.

Dan scraped a hand over his face, shook his head, and mustered up a dry chuckle, blaming the long night shift and apologized for drifting away for a second there.

"I was standing here for a while, man." Pete said, and set the food down on the counter. "You sure you're okay?"

Dan hadn't heard Pete pass through the creaky saloon doors of the kitchen, or the heavy stomp of the Doc Martens he always wore.

How long was I out? He thought.

Pete plucked the Monster Factory card from the counter and turned it over in his hand. His frown deepened.

"Hey." Dan snapped, as he reached for the card, a little too fast.

"This yours?" Pete asked.

"Yeah." Dan said, as he snatched the card from Pete's fingers and replaced it gently back into the billfold of his wallet. "It's my kid's."

The fluorescent lighting in the diner was shit. It bathed everyone in a sickly, yellow glow of jaundice, but Dan looked worse than most. Dark bags hung beneath his eyes the color of old bruises. His skin was stretched too tight over the sharp bones of his skull.

"Yeah, man. Sure." Pete said. "My niece plays that game. Or she used to. I can't keep up anymore. I'm more of a *Call of Duty* man myself."

Dan nodded politely and felt his heartbeat slowly shift down through the gears, as it returned to normal, slowing from rapid canon fire in his ears to a steady bass drum rhythm.

When his radio crackled Dan flinched, he had left the volume too high and the booming dispatcher's voice flooded the quiet space.

"223 Echo, 933?"

"Sorry." Dan mumbled and lowered the volume before he pressed the TALK button on his radio.

"Go ahead."

"Respond to 675 Winston Drive for a welfare check.

Complainant hasn't heard from their upstairs neighbor in quite some time and now there's a weird smell coming from her apartment. We have an ambulance en route as well."

Dan groaned and saw Pete wrinkle his nose.

"Dead body?" Pete asked.

"Probably."

"Shitty, man."

"Yup."

And then into his radio Dan said, "Ten-four."

"How much do I owe you?"

But Pete waved him off, and left Dan holding his wallet.

"Just eat it before you have to deal with…whatever's in that house. I got a feeling you might not be hungry afterwards."

Dan told Pete he would, gathered up his paper sack and his can of Coke, and jogged through the driving rain to his cruiser.

He set his lunch on the passenger seat and knew he wouldn't be eating a bite of it. Not ever. His hunger had been replaced by a roiling ball of bile.

He jammed the key in the ignition and the engine growled to life.

I want you to have it.

His computer terminal attached to the dashboard flickered to life, throwing a pale blue light over the car's interior. Shadows scurried away from the glow and movement in the backseat drew Dan's eyes to the rearview mirror.

The doors were locked. There was no one there. Still, he swivelled in his seat and peered through the plexiglass barrier.

And hoped.

CHAPTER
SIX

The Avernus family lived in a modest two-story bungalow on a pleasant tree lined street, in a neighborhood about twenty years past its prime.

Gone were most of the manicured lawns, and the flower boxes overflowing with blooms of red and blue and gold. A silent army of weeds had infiltrated the carefully tended, square patches of grass and had erupted through the cracks in the sidewalks, quickly claiming more and more territory as their own.

Car parts left to rust in the rain vastly outnumbered the once beautifully carved topiaries.

Some of the houses that had been abandoned, left vacant and surrendered to the bank, had been boarded up against the growing collective of shambling homeless.

A faded FOR SALE sign stood at a lazy angle on the

front lawn of the Avernus home, as if even the sign had given up.

However, warm light glowed from a first floor window, which revealed a small, but tidy living room decorated in natural tones of beige and cream and green.

Inside, Sarah Avernus sat on the edge of her tired cream couch, a glass of bargain basement Riesling at her elbow. The bottle of wine, even this level of quality, was supposed to be saved for special occasions as times were tight, and belts had to be tightened and all that. But if that was the rule, the bottle would dry up and evaporate before the cork was ever popped. Or in this case, the resealable cap twisted off.

After the death of her son, Sean, there were no more good days.

She took a sip and grimaced. The cheap wine had a syrupy feel in her mouth and an aftertaste that reminded her of gasoline. Still, it did its job, and with every swallow she felt a little warmer. Her focus pleasantly blurred around the edges and she felt her chest loosen, the iron grip of anxiety and depression relaxing just enough so she could breathe normally, at least for a little while.

In and out...in and out...

She held her wineglass between her cupped hands and closed her eyes.

It had been five months since his death. Five months of counselling, both with Dan and alone, and with Rose.

Poor Rose.

Sarah pushed the thought of her living daughter away from her mind, as if including her might diminish her light somehow.

Sarah had endured countless hours of therapy rolling quickly through the stages of grief: denial, bargaining, depression, anger, only to stop short on acceptance.

To Sarah, acceptance meant moving on. It meant smiling and not feeling guilty. It meant being happy, and living your life, and enjoying the sunshine, and snowflakes, and everything else the world had to offer. All while your beautiful ten-year-old son was left to rot in a horrifically small coffin under six feet of cold earth, a couple of miles away from his warm bed.

From his home.

From his family.

Sarah lingered for a long time on anger. Hitting it hard. Kicking and punching and clawing at the furious rage that swelled in her chest.

She railed against a God that would steal her son away. That would allow the corruption, the *filth* of cancer, to bloom inside his tiny body. A God that would stand by and let her watch as the sickness spread like a brushfire inside him, devouring his organs from the inside. Leaving him hollowed out. A husk. A skeletal, hairless ghost, with translucent skin, surrounded by a sentinel of wheezing, and softly beeping machines that struggled to keep him alive.

She took another sip of the horrific wine with her

eyes closed and drained the glass. When she opened her eyes she felt no better. Only more tired.

Sarah set the wineglass down on the coffee table and dug into the basket of still warm laundry at her feet. She had found that if she kept herself busy with household chores the dark thoughts could be kept at bay. Not banished. Not gone. But held at the perimeter of her mind, where they existed as barely glimpsed shadows, seen only in the corner of her eye. Waiting for her defenses to fall.

A neatly folded pile of clothes for each member of her family...*each living member*...her mind whispered... grew as she sifted through Dan's t-shirts and folded Rose's overalls, the ones embroidered with a cluster of hearts on the front. She focused on the monotony, enjoying the mindless distraction of sorting underwear and finding matches for errant socks until her fingers plucked a soft, blue t-shirt from the bottom of the basket.

Sean's t-shirt.

Confused, she stared at the garment as if she had found a cactus in the laundry basket.

How did it...

It didn't matter how it got there, she thought. Maybe Rose had crept into her brother's room and had taken it from his drawers, wearing it secretly beneath her clothes. Her version of mourning. Or remembrance.

Sarah couldn't breathe. Just holding the tiny shirt in her hands was enough to break her walls down. She felt the ghostly invaders, who had been waiting for this moment, steal across her mind, dragging all the memories of Sean back to the forefront.

She remembered how excited he was to get the t-shirt while they were on vacation in Myrtle Beach. The faded, grinning skeleton on the front of the shirt was Mr. Bones, the mascot of a Mexican restaurant that treated Sean and Rose like royalty. Bringing their near bursting burritos to the table with a flourish, accompanied by their huge kid-friendly drinks bristling with fruit and colorful umbrellas.

Sarah held the shirt reverently in her hands like a rare artifact. She pressed the soft cotton to her nose, trying to breathe in that last little bit of his scent. But it was gone. It was just a shirt now and the only scent was the cloying smell of artificial lavender.

She folded the shirt into a neat square and placed it in a pile all its own. When she was finished, she reloaded the laundry basket and made her way up the stairs to the second floor.

CHAPTER

SEVEN

At the top of the stairs Sarah found herself at a T intersection where her upstairs hall ran east and west. She turned right and stopped at the first door on her left.

The bedroom door was plastered with KEEP OUT signs and pencil drawings of hockey players and super-heroes. Sidney Crosby, Connor McDavid and Austin Matthews fought for the puck alongside drawings of *Iron Man* and the *Hulk*.

Sean's room.

With a deep breath she twisted the door handle and stepped inside.

She moved through the boy's neat, empty room to a tall dresser that stood next to the window overlooking the

39

front yard and State Street beyond. She pulled out the second drawer from the top and carefully placed the folded Mr. Bones t-shirt inside.

Just go. Her mind whispered. *Get out.*

Sarah eased the drawer closed, and still holding her breath, she turned to inspect the empty single bed draped in a Marvel themed bedspread and the shelves of toys gathering dust. A baseball glove sat on a bedside table, where a battered baseball was left abandoned, peeking out from the pocket.

She didn't leave. Soon she was moving through the room, as she examined each framed photo and drawing tacked to the wall as if she were in a museum exhibit.

And that's what it is. Her mind hissed. *Step right up! Come see the room left behind by a dead boy.*

Sarah ignored the tears that rolled down her hollowed cheeks as she stopped at each picture and her heart broke all over again, and again and again. Every time she saw Sean's crooked smile, and his pale blue eyes the color of denim, exactly like his father's.

The boy was smiling in every picture. Not sullen or distracted, but smiling. *Beaming.* The very definition of good natured, of health and vitality.

The breath she held, burned in her lungs and she finally ripped herself away from the pictures of her smiling dead son.

Sarah scooped up the laundry basket, ripped open the bedroom door and burst into the hall. She slammed the door behind her hard enough to rattle the framed family portraits hung along the hall. She gasped as she struggled to suck in a breath and felt her heartbeat pound in her temples.

She drew in deep lungfuls of air as her chest hitched and a flood of tears threatened to sweep her into another black hole of depression. She blinked and straightened her shoulders against the coming storm. She gripped the handle of the laundry basket, and relished the painful pinch as the cracked edge of the plastic hamper dug its plastic claw into her right hip.

The pain brought her back to the hall. To the here and now. She was still a mother. Still a wife. She still had a job to do. A duty to fulfill. She could not fall apart.

She would deliver the rest of these clothes to their owners and maybe take a bath before bed. It had been a while since she soaked in the tub. And maybe only one Valium before she slipped between the sheets and prayed for sleep.

No more than two. Her mind whispered. *Not again.*

As Sarah tip-toed toward her daughter's bedroom at the end of the hall, she heard the sound of Rose's muffled voice. It was after midnight on a school night, three hours past her bedtime. She should have been asleep by now.

Sarah arrived at Rose's closed bedroom door and set the laundry basket on the floor. Like her brother's, Rose's door was decorated. However, Rose favored flowers over drawings and as a result her entire door was covered in a lush garden made of delicate paper flowers of every variation. Carefully crafted daisies, roses, and violets shared space with huge, brilliant yellow sunflowers.

Each one lovingly cut from construction paper, painstakingly assembled on their kitchen table and strategically stapled onto a piece of thick, green astroturf. The result was a magical rectangle of garden tilted ninety-degrees, complete with a doorknob painted to look like a bright red mushroom cap from the *Super Mario Bros.* video game.

Sarah stood close to the door, and pressed her cheek against the paper daffodils, and listened. She heard her daughter's whispered voice but couldn't discern any words. The cadence stopped and started as if she were in the midst of a conversation.

Rose had asked them for a cell phone before her twelfth birthday, but she and Dan had vetoed the request. Personally, Sarah didn't have any objections, but it was Dan who had put his foot down citing all the horrible police calls involving teens and cell phones, and argued for them to wait another year before allowing the world a portal into their home. A private channel to their only daughter.

Sarah gripped the red mushroom cap dotted with white, and twisted. The door swung inward, and the hushed sound of Rose's voice went silent.

$\sim$

THE ROOM WAS DARK, lit only by the diffused, yellow light of a streetlamp outside her window. Still, Sarah saw the posters advertising a video game character called *Cherry Pain,* an avatar players could use in her latest video game obsession, *Dead by Dawn.*

Cherry was a long and lean, stylized and barely clothed teen girl, with two black ponytails that were long enough to be horse tails. She was in the midst of a jump straight off the paper of the poster, a steampunk version of a six-shooter gripped in each hand.

Rose's bed was empty. The sheets were twisted in a snarl near the footboard. The pillow left abandoned in the middle of the bed.

"I know." Rose whispered. "I heard you."

Her voice was coming from beneath the bed.

Sarah slowly lowered herself to the floor and found her daughter's skinny bare legs sticking out of her pale, white nightdress, dotted with embroidered flowers. Her black hair was pooled around her face, her tiny white hands pillowed beneath her chin.

"I told you she was here." She whispered, "I gotta go...*I will.* I said I will, *gosh.*"

Sarah scooted backwards across the hardwood floor as Rose crawled out from beneath the bed. She clawed at the long strands of hair that covered her beautiful face and then blew the last strand away from her nose with a puff of air.

"Hey, Mom."

A smile, one of the few genuine smiles she could

remember lately, flickered across Sarah's dry lips as she watched Rose. Her daughter crawled into a seated position across from her, her legs crossed. Soon she would be too big to slip under the bed. Even now her head barely fit. *She could thank her Dad for that,* Sarah thought.

"A little late, don't you think, Rosie? It's after midnight."

Rose's smooth, pale skin beamed in the watery yellow light.

"It's not me, Mom. It's not my fault." She whispered. "He woke me up."

"You're still talking to him?"

Rose nodded, suddenly guilty, as if she had done something wrong.

Since the death of her brother, Rose had been *speaking* to Sean. Her grief counsellor suggested it was a way for her to cope with the loss, and let it run its natural course. Neither Dan nor Sarah encouraged it, but it had been going on for months now, and it wasn't going away.

"It's okay, honey." Sarah told her. "I won't get upset. I wish I could talk to him."

"You do?" Rosie beamed.

Sarah nodded, desperate not to cry again.

"What's he saying?"

Rose scrunched up her face and asked, "Can I say a bad word?"

Sarah nodded and braced herself.

"He's being *stupid.*"

Sarah tried her best to look dutifully aghast at Rosie's choice of curse word as she said, "Why is that?"

"He says we have to go home. But we are home." Rose said, her delicate features pinched with irritation. "I keep telling him, but he won't listen. He keeps saying the same thing."

Sarah stared at her daughter, studying her eyes for the lie that wasn't there.

Was she really talking to Sean?

Could she really hear him?

Of course not.

"Come on, honey." Sarah said finally. "Time for bed. For real this time."

Sarah pulled her daughter into a hug and lifted her off the floor. She carried her the three steps to her bed and set her down gently. Sarah placed the pillow under her head, and straightened out the tangle of blankets, and drew them up to Rose's chin.

"Close your eyes, okay." Sarah said, and dropped a kiss on her forehead. "It's really late. Don't wanna be grumpy for school tomorrow."

Sarah was at the door, nearly across the threshold when Rose whispered from the shadows of her room, "He's not sick anymore, Mom. He's not."

Sarah froze, afraid to turn around. Afraid Rose would say something else. Without facing her daughter Sarah mumbled, "Get some sleep." And dragged the door closed behind her.

. . .

DOWNSTAIRS, Sarah poured the last of the terrible wine into her glass and then rifled through her purse until she found her prescription bottle of Valium.

She chased one pill with a swallow of wine, then added another one for good measure and prayed for oblivion.

EIGHT

Dan had driven past the address twice, he was sure of it. The rain had let up, but it still screened the dark houses in a shifting veil. He pulled to the curb, stepped out into the rain, and snapped on his flashlight.

The address he was sent to was in a neighborhood nicknamed, *Silvertown*, by the locals. It consisted of ancient brick row houses sandwiched together on either side of narrow streets. On Winston Drive no lights burned in the windows he could see, and most windows were shattered or missing all together.

About a hundred feet from his cruiser, his flashlight found his destination: 675 Winston Drive. The address had originally been stamped into the brickwork, but the stone was chipped and the numbers were barely legible now.

Dan climbed the three steps up to the stamp-sized concrete porch. He peered into the small, grimy windows set into the door once painted a dark brown or black. Curls of paint peeled from the door and formed a greasy pile at his feet.

He poked his flashlight through the window smeared with dirt and dust and saw no movement. No lights. There was no buzzer to be found, so he knocked. First neighbourly, and then much harder, kicking the bottom edge of the door with the toe of his patrol boot. The solid wood door rattled in its frame, and showered the concrete with more flecks of dark paint.

When no one answered, he tried the handle and to his surprise the knob twisted easily in his grasp. He pushed the door inward and the unmistakable stench of a rotting corpse drifted out to meet him, along with a horde of buzzing flies.

Dan swore, shifted back a few steps, and covered his mouth with his hand. There was no smell like that of a dead body, and after the first few weeks of patrol, one recognized it instantly. A cloying rotten reek. The stench of coagulating bodily fluids, fresh human waste and the sickly-sweet scent of what was once a person, slowly melting into a hideous puddle, peppered with bone.

After a few deep breaths, Dan stepped across the threshold, left the door open wide behind him and found himself in a small foyer.

Two steps in another smell fought for dominance: Mold. Newspapers, magazines, and books were piled in crooked stacks of six foot high towers. A winding, narrow path had been left providing access deeper into the home. Dan's beam found a yellowed light switch, caked with a film of nicotine, and dared it to work. No such luck.

"Of course." He muttered and moved deeper into the stacks. His broad shoulders brushed the nearby towers on either side and caused them to bend and sway.

He followed the path through what used to be a living room, now a warehouse filled with knick knacks. Boxes of chipped porcelain dolls, and old paperbacks bloated with water damage and scabby with mold.

Still the smell persisted, and Dan pressed on, hoping the dead woman wasn't buried under a fallen stack. He swept his light into a small kitchen. More boxes of useless shit, more books and magazines decades old.

Here at least the stove was clear of clutter. The sink, on the other hand, was piled high with dirty dishes. The scraps of food long since fossilized had grown furry with mold. Maggots writhed in ecstasy on a plate left near the stove. The remains of a pork chop were barely visible beneath the squirming legion.

Dan checked the remaining ground floor rooms: a two-piece bathroom and a walk-in pantry, and found no one.

He stopped at the foot of the narrow wooden stairs leading to the second floor and waited.

She would be up there. He was certain. As he stood there waiting, he could almost see the fog of death rolling down the stairs to greet him.

He swore again and trudged up the risers. *I should've been a fireman*, he thought.

Photographs of a stern looking family. Mother,

father, and little daughter adorned the wall on his way up. In each photo the subjects got a little older.

In the first photo, near the bottom of the stairs everyone was wearing purple turtlenecks. The barely teenaged daughter wore a daisy behind her ear, and she was the only one smiling. Dan saw that the girl lost more and more of her smile as the years passed in the pictures. The last one, the parents stood alone. Both looking like they would rather be somewhere else.

Dan wondered what happened to the girl.

He topped the stairs and movement to his left pulled his head around. He shined his light down the long hall that ended in what looked like a bedroom doorway.

The beam of his flashlight played over the empty doorframe, and he saw the corner of a green bedspread and a small bedside table through the gap. But he could have sworn that he saw someone walk past the open door.

Frozen at the top of the steps, Dan called out, his voice sounding a lot weaker than he would have liked.

"Hello?" He said, a little breathlessly. "Police. Anyone there?"

Rain tapped on the windows and hammered the metal roof. He even heard some of the deluge trickling behind the walls and thought the basement was probably a filthy swimming pool.

"Hello?" He called again.

He played the light over the doorway again, as his right hand crept up to the grip of his pistol.

Silvertown had a huge number of vacant properties

and the homeless community seized on them. Especially ones with oblivious, elderly, or easily intimidated owners. *Who knew how many squatters had built a nest up here?*

Again, his light twitched over the end of the hall, over the green bedspread and the polished wood end table in the bedroom.

He should have called for backup.

A little late now, he thought.

The window behind him flickered with blue and red flashing lights. He looked down to the street and saw an ambulance pulling in and watched it park against the curb, its emergency lights splashing colour over the monochrome scene below.

Soon the paramedics would call out to him, as they edged through the warren of moldy circulars to the creaky old stairs that belonged in a cheesy horror movie from the sixties. There would be smiles and jokes about the smell, the hoarding, et cetera. He wouldn't be alone for long.

If she was alive, he and the paramedics would corral the old woman shuffling around up here and take her to the hospital.

If she was alive.

Still, he had to find her first.

Dan left the top of the stairs and started making his way down the gloomy hallway. The first door to his right was a child's bedroom. It held a narrow single bed, a chest of drawers and a small writing desk. The walls were painted a light pink. The floor was left clear of any boxes, books, or moldy towers. Besides the obvious buildup of dust in the years it lay vacant, the room was pristine.

He wondered if the girl in the photographs had died. Maybe that's why her childhood room was untouched. Maybe that, the death of their child, drove this woman mad. Triggered her hoarding. Her life of neglect.

A sound somewhere to his left brought him back to the present. A scrape. A shuffle. A quick burst of light footsteps.

Someone was up here.

Next was a small bathroom. Every surface was coated in a layer of dust or decay. Grungy and dirty. A dense cloud of buzzing flies swarmed over the toilet splattered with feces. The toilet seat he noticed, was missing. The pale blue floor tiles were stained with years of dried urine.

He heard a door slam downstairs and someone hissed, "*Jesus Christ.*"

Dan smiled and pushed on to the final door. The master bedroom. The room where he saw movement.

At the doorway he called out again, "Hello?"

Still nothing. No response.

But the smell was definitely worse here. Dan was forced to cover his mouth as he edged closer.

The madness that he had walked through downstairs seemed to have started here. Crumbling cardboard boxes were stacked nearly to the ceiling in moldering towers. Books, magazines, and newspapers covered the floor.

The police-issued flashlights had two major design

flaws: The first, was that they were small and cheap and heated up hotter than the July sun after a few short minutes. The second, was the batteries. Standing there at the threshold, Dan shifted the uncomfortably warm flashlight to his opposite hand as the beam flickered and died.

Darkness flooded into the hallway, which left only a veiled square of moonlight at the opposite end of the passage. Dan tapped at the flashlight and checked his pockets for spare batteries, but he was out.

He heard the shuffle scrape of a footstep inside the dark room and froze, his breath caught in his chest.

The silence expanded.

CHAPTER

NINE

Dan tapped the flashlight again and the beam returned, slightly weakened.

"Hello?" Dan said, as he slipped into the bedroom. "Police."

Another sound, this one closer. Wet footsteps slapped on the floor covered in old paper. Dan's light flickered again as he stepped deeper into the bedroom, shining his light around the delicately balanced towers of old *National Geographics* and ancient copies of *Reader's Digest.*

He followed the curved path through the stacks until his light found the figure of an old man. He was average height, and he stood facing the corner of the bedroom, his gray head bowed. Dan heard the muffled buzz of the man's whispered voice as he spoke to himself, as if in prayer.

He wore a dark rain slicker, jeans and rubber boots. Every item of clothing was streaked with mud, scuffed and tattered, as if the man had been dragged behind a truck. At his feet, his sodden clothes formed a puddle of brackish water. He appeared to Dan as a drowned fisherman, plucked from the depths of the sea and, for reasons unknown, teleported to this very room.

Dan slipped his hand over the grip of his pistol and released the first safety catch which kept the gun in its holster.

"Hey, man." Dan said. "I need you to turn around, real slow, okay? Nice and easy."

Dan's light flickered and strobed pulses of white, and then, faded to nothing.

"Shit."

In the darkness Dan heard the man shuffle in place. His heavy boots squeaked on the wet floor, ripping through old newspaper as he turned to face him.

A strangled voice, more of a growl, than anything resembling human speech issued from the dark. Two words hissed across the expanse.

"Come...home..."

Dan slapped the flashlight as he shuffled backward, and bumped into a stack of old books.

The voice again, rumbled out of the shadows, a lion's roar as heavy footsteps thundered toward him.

"COME HOME!"

Dan's light returned for one last flash and in that moment, Dan saw the face of the homeless man. The lost fisherman.

The old man's eyes had been gouged from his head. From every orifice of his face, black tendrils, like voracious vines, twisted hungrily across his flesh and sprouted from his dirty gray beard.

His filthy hands were hooked into claws, desperate to rip Dan apart, as he charged across the short distance between them. Inches away, Dan could taste the man's rancid breath as they collided in a tangle of limbs.

Dan stumbled backward and dropped the useless flashlight, as he ripped his pistol from the holster. His back struck a tower of ancient newspapers and the entire stack collapsed on top of him in an avalanche of rotten newsprint.

He screamed and writhed, trapped under the man's dead weight, as he struggled to aim the barrel of his gun at the target.

The floor vibrated with rushing footsteps as twin beams of light cut through the gloom.

"Dan?" A voice called. "Dan is that you?"

Dan cleared away the newspaper that had covered his face and stared into a pair of flashlight beams.

"Jesus, you all right?"

Dan recognized the voice. It belonged to Eddie Freeman. A chubby, bald, paramedic he had known since joining the force.

Even without hearing the voice he could tell it was Eddie from the smell of his ever present cinnamon gum. A defense mechanism he employed against the horrible scents of his day to day.

For a moment Dan lay there, waiting. What for exactly, he didn't know. After a moment, he noticed his gun was out and still in his hand. He could feel his heart hammering in his ears, but it was slowing.

"We heard you yell...so." Eddie's partner said, a young woman Dan didn't recognize.

Dan struggled to his knees, and finally to his feet, brushing away the bits of wet paper that clung to his uniform, and carefully returned his weapon to its holster.

"There was a guy in here." He told them. "You didn't see him? On the stairs maybe?"

The paramedics shared a glance, shrugged, and then turned back to Dan, as their lights probed the corners of the bedroom.

"Nah, man." Eddie said. "Just you."

As Eddie helped him to his feet, Dan could feel the other man's eyes on him, the concern on his face. The worry.

"Let me see your light." Dan said, and used Eddie's flashlight to find the spot in the corner where the man had stood. An oval puddle of dirty water remained, but any sign of the man was gone.

Eddie crept up beside Dan and whispered, "You sure you're all right, man?"

No. He was not all right. He had seen the man. He had smelled and felt the man as he tackled him. Worst of all, Dan recognized him.

"Dan?" Eddie asked again. "You good?"

Before he could answer, Eddie's partner called out, "Found her."

Without another word, Eddie and Dan carefully

picked their way through the wreckage, to the far corner of the bedroom.

Hidden by a short wall constructed of crumbling boxes and bloated encyclopedias was the withered, nearly mummified corpse, of an elderly woman. Her head lay tilted against the headrest of the armchair, her frosted gaze aimed at a window overlooking the street. Her skin was the greasy black of old bananas, and what remained of her internal organs had long since melted into the fabric of the chair.

Eddie's young partner caught a whiff of the liquifying woman and Dan saw her head snap back as if she were slapped. She put a gloved hand to her nose and mumbled something before she hurried away toward the hall.

Dan wandered back across the room where he had seen the man that attacked him as Eddie shuffled after his young partner.

In the hall, Dan could hear the young paramedic as she dry heaved and Eddie told her to focus on her breathing.

The fisherman's image was burned in his brain. The entire encounter, as brief as it was, played on a loop. The wet clothes, the greedy black tendrils that snaked from his eyes and mouth.

That voice.

He remembered that voice. He remembered the pain and disappointment, and fury baked into every word the last time he heard it. He remembered his father turning his back on him as he stood at the door of his old Ford Ranger.

Dan remembered the last words his father said to him, and the old anger sparked to life deep in the boiler of his chest. Tongues of flame fed on years of dry kindling, and as the fire grew, Dan felt his hands curl into fists.

Maybe it was too soon to come back. Maybe he wasn't as ready as he thought he was. Maybe he should have stuck with therapy like Sarah.

Dan's eyes were fixed on the dirty puddle left behind by the fisherman when Eddie appeared at his side.

"If you're good here, Dan, we're gonna clear."

Dan nodded and handed Eddie his light.

"How's she doing?" Dan asked.

"Puking up the last of her burrito, but she'll be all right." Eddie said. "Everybody remembers their first, right? You sure you're good?"

"Yeah." Dan told him, and dredged up a small smile. "A little embarrassed, is all."

Eddie shrugged, "Could've been worse. Besides, you always were a spaz."

Dan chuckled and said, "And I remember you being funnier."

Eddie glanced at his watch, "This close to home time after a twelve hour shift, you're lucky I'm still speaking English. Anyways, body removal is on the way. Should be here within the hour. You want us to stay?"

Dan shook his head.

"Nah, you guys take off. I'm just gonna sit in the cruiser, catch up on some notes."

"All right, man." Eddie said. "Get home safe."

For a few minutes more Dan stood in the darkness of the bedroom listening to the pounding rain as the storm gathered strength while his father's words played on a loop in his mind.

Come home

TEN

OAK BAY, OREGON

nderson Seville looked about as out of place in Marcus Avernus' country kitchen as Chris Rock at a Klan rally.

He was tall and sleek, and reminded Ruth of an otter standing upright, right down to the slicked back chestnut hair and the slightly protruding front teeth. She smiled into her tea, and he stopped pacing to glare at her.

"Something funny, Ruth?" He snapped. "'Cause I am certainly not in on the fucking joke. Do you have any idea what this means?" Ruth shook her head and mumbled her apology, then took another sip of the lukewarm chamomile as Anderson stomped past a wooden rack of collectible spoons and fumed. He had not stopped pacing since his arrival late this morning.

She remembered how the man had strutted up the steps of her home and had swept inside without so much as a courtesy knock. The delicate features of his face arranged in its default expression of smug arrogance.

She remembered how his icy stare searched the corners of their tiny kitchen for Marcus, and barely acknowledged that she was sitting right in front of him, until his search came up empty.

"He's not answering my calls." He had said, in his clipped, slightly effeminate voice. "My texts, emails. Where is he, Ruth?"

"He's gone." She had told him flatly. "Missing."

THAT WAS twelve minutes ago if the clock above the stove was correct. And still, twelve minutes later, he paced and wore a rut in the creaky floorboards, as his manicured hands flexed and curled into fists ready to strangle someone. *Anyone.*

He continued to ask the same question in a variety of colorful ways.

"What the fuck do you mean he's *gone*?"

Ruth set down the blueberry scone she had been nibbling on and met his gaze.

"I can only tell you what I know, Anderson."

"Tell me again." He said.

Anderson actually stopped pacing for a moment and pulled out the kitchen chair opposite Ruth. He studied the worn seat and the white paint chipping from the spindles of the backrest, winced, and pushed the chair back under the table.

"Go ahead."

"He left last night for the island and hasn't returned." She told him.

"What the fuck was he doing going to the island at night? Why would he do that?"

Ruth knew this question was coming. She had had to answer it this morning when she finally called the Sheriff's Office to report Marcus missing. She didn't know how to bluff. She had a horrible poker face and it showed as she forced out the same simple lie she had told Sheriff Roberts.

"I don't know, Anderson."

Anderson paused for a second and stared at her as if the word LIAR suddenly appeared across her forehead in red neon.

For a moment, she could feel his eyes on her like a physical weight, probing. Finally, Anderson pursed his thin lips as he contemplated something, rejected it almost instantly, and then resumed his pacing.

Ruth waited for him to turn his back on her to let out the breath she was holding.

"The Kaminskis are flying in next week." He said. "What the hell am I supposed to tell them?"

"You can tell them the truth." She muttered.

Anderson barked out a high-pitched laugh that sounded like the strangled yelp of a small dog.

"The truth? Are you serious?" He said. "You want me to tell them that a multi-million dollar deal, *a multi-billion dollar development*, is now in the shitter because the owner has gone AWOL? You think your little island is the only one these guys are scouting?"

"I don't know, Anderson."

"Well, spoiler alert, it's not, *Ruth*." He told her. "These brothers probably have a short list of at least five others with owners who haven't *fucking disappeared!*"

"Enough!" Ruth snapped.

The flat of her hand slammed down on the kitchen table hard enough to rattle the ceramic penguin salt and pepper shakers in their holder.

She fixed her blue eyes on Anderson and pinned the younger man in place.

"I know you're upset. I do." She said. "But Marcus is *missing. Missing, Anderson.* I know him better than you do. He didn't disappear. Or run away. Something has happened. And right now, that takes priority over anything else."

She felt tears burning the backs of her eyes and back-handed them away.

Anderson wiped the edge of the counter with one hand, and after he deemed it suitably clean, he leaned against it, and crossed his arms over his narrow chest. Ruth went back to her scone and broke off a tiny piece before she chewed it slowly.

"Well, did he say anything? You know, before he left?"

"Jesus Christ, Anderson!" Ruth said.

"Well, what?" He said, as he threw his hands in the air. "Did he?"

Ruth shook her head, not wanting to risk saying something else that would, no doubt, incriminate her.

"No, Anderson. Okay?" Ruth told him.

"He just up and left. And you let him?"

Ruth's glare hit Anderson like a lash, and he immediately looked away.

"I'm not his mother, Anderson." She said. "He's a grown man. All I know is that he took the fishing boat out last night and he didn't come back."

"Well, did you call the Sheriff?"

"This morning."

"And?"

"And they're not back yet either."

Anderson pushed off the counter and trudged over the floorboards to the kitchen door. He looked like he wanted to punch something. Instead, he plucked his camel's hair coat from the hook and shoved his arms into the sleeves.

"Fuck!" He hissed. "Fuck."

He pushed through the creaky kitchen door and stepped out onto the porch pulling a slim vape pen from a pocket of his coat.

The door swung shut behind him, but Ruth could still see him through the window. He hauled on the thin white tube and exhaled a cottony cloud of smoke that would no doubt smell like fabricated peaches or some such nonsense.

She watched him take another long toke and

followed his gaze to the island in the distance, hidden behind a thin veil of fog and whispered a prayer for Marcus' safe return.

CHAPTER

ELEVEN

Sheriff Wayne Roberts of the Oak Bay Police Service sat in the passenger seat behind the wind screen of the *Gypsy*. The *Gypsy* was a late model cabin cruiser that Wayne mostly used for fishing, but when the time came, he loaned it to the Sheriff's office for the tax break and the free gas.

At the helm was his son and Senior Deputy James "Call me Jimmy" Roberts.

After years of icy winters and being on the water in all manner of weather, Wayne had learned to dress in layers and cover up. He took some shit from Jimmy about the Sherpa lined, leather hat he wore with the ear flaps, but Wayne hated being cold and if being warm came at the expense of a few tired jokes, he would make the sacrifice.

The storm that had ripped through their little part of

the world had finally died out and the sea was calm this morning. *Thank God.* The only thing he hated more than being cold was being on a boat in rough water. He doubled that when his son was at the helm. But today the Pacific was as flat as it ever got and the ride out to Avernus Island had so far, been a pleasant one.

The cruiser rose and fell on the swells and instead of bracing himself for every wave that would crash against the bow, he had time to think about the conversation he had with Ruth Coolidge this morning up at the Avernus house.

The call had come in around 7 AM, and Margaret Bleekman, who manned the phones and took care of the Sheriff's Office, said that Ruth sounded worried, but not hysterical. Wayne had grown up with Ruth and knew she wasn't the type to start screaming and wailing unless there was a reason for it.

Margaret had relayed the message to Wayne that Ruth was concerned because Marcus had taken his tiny fishing boat over to the island last night and hadn't returned.

So there they were, the Roberts boys, father and son, up at the Avernus house around eight in the morning. They sat in Marcus' kitchen, crowded around the round wooden breakfast table to hear Ruth's story.

They nibbled on fresh baked blueberry scones and sipped sweet, dark coffee as she went through the events leading to when she last saw Marcus.

Oak Bay was a small seaside community of barely five thousand people. The number swelled a bit in the summer, when the tourists from the interior were determined to spend the summer months on the coast, but for the most part, it was a place where strangers were rare. Everyone knew everyone else, and people usually kept to themselves.

Other than a few fights at Sullivan's, or the occasional domestic, the village of Oak Bay was quiet, and that suited Sheriff Wayne Roberts perfectly.

Ruth's mother, Meryl Coolidge, worked as the Avernus' housekeeper since before Marcus was born. When Meryl's husband, Stanley, got caught up in a crab line and was dragged overboard about a hundred miles offshore, she and little Ruth had moved into the Avernus home.

Years later when Meryl took sick with a spectacularly vicious breed of stomach cancer, Ruth chose to stay and take care of her and oversee her mother's duties inside the Avernus home.

When Meryl died, Ruth decided not to leave the village of Oak Bay, but to stay with the Avernus family; tending to little Marcus and much later, Marcus' own family, especially his son, Daniel.

Ruth was treated as nothing less than family. She was forthright and loyal and always told you the plain truth, even when it hurt. Which bothered Wayne so much, because he knew she was lying to him.

When she was finished telling her story Wayne asked her to go over the days before Marcus' disappearance. Any new stress? New medications? New worries he might have shared with her.

Wayne had heard rumors of rich folks from California or Europe or China, coming to buy the island and put up condos. But if he had a nickel for every time someone floated that rumor down at Sullivan's, he wouldn't be bouncing along in the goddamn police boat, having his balls batted against the frozen plastic seat, that's for sure.

Ruth denied any such dealings with mysterious investors, and she reiterated that she had no idea why Marcus had gone out that night. She had tried to stop him of course, because it was getting dark and a storm was rolling in, but he wouldn't listen.

Nothing about her story made sense to the lawman.

Why would a solid guy like Marcus Avernus go for a twilight boat ride to a deserted island?

No reason came to mind.

Still, until there was something to worry about, Wayne was of the mindset to not worry. Marcus' behaviour was a bit weird, yes. A bit out of character? Of course. But still, Wayne was confident that they would land on the island and find Marcus had run out of gas or his boat had floated away, or at worse, he was nursing a broken leg up by the barracks, waiting to be rescued.

All would be fine, and in a few days, Marcus would buy a few rounds down at the pub and they would all have a good laugh.

Except Wayne's bullshit detector was legendary, and he could smell the lie on Ruth as easily as if she were dipped in pig shit.

Why would Ruth lie?

Was she covering for him? Did she do something to him?

It nagged at Wayne.

"We're here, Dad." Jimmy said.

Wayne looked up, and through the windshield splattered with streaks of water, he saw the dark, rocky beach of Avernus Island rising into view.

CHAPTER

TWELVE

Jimmy eased the throttle back to nothing and let the boat drift into the sand bar next to Marcus' old fishing boat.

They heard the crunch and scrape of the hull grind into the sand and bits of rock and then young Jimmy was over the bow with the tow rope in his hands before Wayne could climb to his feet.

He watched his son loop a length of rope around a jutting bit of rock and tie a loose knot, and he felt something strange in his chest. His right hand moved to his sternum and massaged a spot below his heart.

Pressure.

He stared at his son walking back to the boat, a puzzled look on his face, and felt something pressing down on him, from every angle. He couldn't breathe.

"You coming old man?" Jimmy said.

Wayne forced out a chuckle and struggled to his feet. He felt like he was breathing through a straw.

"I'm coming, goddamn it."

As Wayne stood the boat settled deeper in the sand and tilted at an odd angle. Black spots swam across his vision and Wayne lost his footing. He stumbled backward and was dumped back into his seat. Jimmy tried to cover his grin with his glove, but couldn't quite hide it. Wayne cursed and scrambled to his feet.

"Say something." Wayne told him. "See how fucking funny it is when you gotta swim back."

"Come on, now, old timer." Jimmy said and held out his hand. "Let me help you."

Wayne grabbed the side rail of the boat and hauled himself to the edge, as he waved away his son's outstretched hand.

"Get that hand away." He said. "I ain't no cripple."

The Sheriff set one boot up on the rail and in one fluid movement, jumped down onto the sand. He landed hard, but he stuck the landing, and he did his best to hide the flash of pain that sparked in his knees.

"Goddamn, pops." Jimmy cried. "Look at you, like a geriatric *Spider-Man.*"

Wayne straightened and shuffled over to Marcus' boat left tethered to the shore, which gave him time to focus on his breathing.

"*Geriatric, my ass.*" He muttered.

He turned away from his son and slowly felt the invisible iron vise around his chest begin to loosen.

Thank God.

Wayne blinked and after realizing that he was going to live for a little while longer and not die of a massive heart attack right here on the beach, focused on the task at hand.

Marcus' boat was empty, except for the rainwater that damn near filled it. The only things left inside were a single oar and an ancient life preserver that floated on the surface that used to be red, but had been bleached by the sun and was now bone-white.

Wayne studied the motor and, without starting the thing, thought it looked good. No obvious damage. He reached into the freezing cold water trapped in the boat and unclipped the red plastic gas can. He shook it and saw it was still about half full. He set it down next to the boat and turned to his son, who was digging a pack of cigarettes from a zippered pocket.

"Don't make no sense." Wayne said.

"What'chu thinking?" Jimmy said, as he slipped a cigarette between his lips. He snapped a silver zippo between the fingers of his right hand igniting a two-inch flame.

"First off, I think Ruth is full of shit." Wayne told him.

Jimmy blew out a cloud of smoke and nodded.

"She sure did look a little cagey."

"Cagey my ass." Wayne grumbled. "She was lying right to my face. She knows why he came out here. She knows exactly why, she just doesn't want to tell us yet."

"And why is that, you think?"

"The hell if I know." Wayne said and raked his scowl across the rocky beach. "Why the hell would anyone want to come out here? Especially at night? Place gives me the creeps."

Wayne turned his sour look toward his son as he shuffled up through the bits of shale to stand next to him.

"Wish you would quit those things." He told him, waving away the cloud of smoke as he passed through.

"I will when you do." Jimmy said, and offered the pack to his father.

Wayne pulled one from the deck and Jimmy lit it.

"You're supposed to be smarter than me, boy."

"Smarter than you?" Jimmy said with a smile. "I thought that was impossible."

Wayne blew out a column of smoke toward the cement colored sky and grinned.

"Well, you got me there, I guess." He said. "Come on, let's go find this idiot."

"After you."

Wayne nodded and led his son up the beach to the natural opening between two towering columns of stone. He hadn't traveled much in his life. Had never left the country, except to Mexico on his honeymoon, but that was ages ago, but one day bored at the office he began googling rock forests.

He realized that they were rare, but he did find one in Shilin, China. The rocks there were a lot bigger than the ones on Avernus Island, but the idea was the same. A strange formation of stone, almost like stalagmites pushing up through the ground like jagged teeth.

The path cut left and right, and if you weren't careful you could find yourself lost in a blind alley. But Wayne had been here more times than he could count, and could probably get to the clearing with his eyes closed.

"You ever come out here? I mean as a kid?" Jimmy asked.

"As a kid, shit yeah." Wayne replied. "Got my very first...uh, *kiss*, right about where you're standing. Senior year. Greta Little."

"You and Ms. Little?"

Wayne nodded, pitched his cigarette onto the ground and stamped the fire out.

"Ms. Eleanor Little, eh?" Jimmy said. "The chubby old lady that owns the yarn shop in town?"

"She's not that old. We're the same age, and she was a lot skinnier back then, let me tell you. And wild." Wayne told him. "Of course, this was before your mother."

"Damn." Jimmy said. "She's about as big as a house now, wears ripped up crocs on her feet year-round. Drives one of them electric scooters. What do they call them...*rascals*?"

"Yeah," Wayne said and shook his head. "Shit's a shame."

They made their way through winding left hand turns and sharp rights, until they emerged beneath the massive stone arch.

Beyond the wide courtyard the crumbling army barracks loomed above them. Three stories high and shaped like a 'C' on its side, it surrounded the courtyard on three sides.

"Looks like somebody has been here." Jimmy said

and kicked through some assorted trash left by campers and weekend explorers. Wayne nodded, stared up into the barracks' blown out windows. No matter how many warnings he issued to the school kids, no matter how many signs he posted around town that the barracks weren't safe and the island was private property, there were still folks who decided to visit the damn place.

There was even a death a few years back when one YouTuber idiot fell through the top floor of the building. Got his dumbass impaled on a piece of rusted plumbing. Wayne prayed that wasn't the case today.

He shuffled further into the courtyard toward the center. Toward the weird stone well and marvelled, as he did every time he saw its walls made of polished ebony rock. It sat there amid the flattened landscape like a beautiful lone rose. A glossy shadow made whole, except for the god-awful grey capstone. Sloppy and hastily done, it looked like some giant baby had smashed a mud pie on top of the jeweled column and left it there to bake in the sun.

Wayne shook his head until he spotted something positioned near the base of the well. He stepped closer and saw it was a canvas bag hammered nearly flat by the pounding rain. Wayne could see the outline of a hammer against the canvas and there was a pry bar lying beside it, nearly swallowed up by the muddy ground.

THIRTEEN

Wayne squatted and heard his knees pop like pistol cracks.

"Damn." Jimmy said. "I heard those knees from over here."

"Boy, do you ever shut up?"

Wayne teased up the edge of the bag and reached in for the hammer. The letters MA were burned into the smooth wooden handle.

What the hell were you doing out here, Marcus?

Still holding the hammer Wayne straightened and scanned the courtyard again.

"Marcus!" Wayne shouted. His booming voice echoed off the shattered remains of the barracks. "Hey Marcus!"

No one responded.

No birds wheeled above. None perched on the ruins of the barracks. In fact, there was no noise at all, except the constant susurration of the surf crashing on the beach.

Wayne didn't call out a third time. He was hoped they would find him quickly, but if they didn't, they would have to search the barracks. And he wasn't sure he wanted to do that. Not only were they dangerous, but with just the two of them out here it might get dicey if one or both of them got hurt in the process.

Jimmy watched him from the other side of the well.

"I found some of Marcus' tools." Wayne told him.

"What the hell was he doing out here?" Jimmy asked, as he teased another smoke from his pack.

Wayne carried the hammer to the well and examined the capstone. He set the hammer down on the scarred surface. The top was dented and bore fresh wounds. Chips of concrete were missing here and there, and he noticed a small, almost triangular hole near the center. The hole was new.

"When's the last time you were out here?" Wayne asked.

"Couple weeks ago? Chased the Mullen boys out here. They were fucking around in the barracks playing commando or some such shit."

"You remember this hole?"

Jimmy met him at the well and leaned in close as Wayne dug out his flashlight and aimed the light into the hole.

"Nope. Can't say as I do."

"Think the Mullen boys did it?"

"They didn't have any tools when I saw them." Jimmy said."You see anything in there?"

Wayne winced and pulled his head back, away from the hole and snapped off the light.

"Nah." He said, and spat to get the rank taste of rot and sewage out of his mouth. "Stinks like holy hell, though."

"What do you think's down there?"

Wayne shook off the question and scanned the windows of the barracks.

"You think he was out here trying to bust up the cap? Why?" Jimmy asked.

"Jimmy, I have no idea. But we're not going into that bullshit by ourselves."

"The barracks?"

Wayne nodded.

"We're gonna search the courtyard, and the ground floor and then call in a special team from the city. You remember what happened to that YouTube fella?"

Jimmy nodded and shot a glance at the west side of the building where he had found the body. Wayne followed his gaze.

"You see someone?"

Jimmy shook his head.

"Nah...It's just...this place." He said. "It always gives me the creeps. Don't know how those Mullen boys could run around here without a care in the world. I fucking hate coming here."

Wayne clapped the boy on his shoulder and gave him a squeeze.

"Then let's get this done, then, yeah?"

Wayne called out again, "MARCUS! *MARCUS!*"

Anger rose in his voice now, mixed with a little fear. From experience Wayne knew that the longer Marcus was missing, especially a guy his age, the less of a chance there was of a positive outcome.

Wayne glared at the shattered windows of the barracks and listened to the echo of his voice fade away with no return. He swore and his breath clouded the air around his face. The temperature had dropped since they arrived.

Where the hell are you, Marcus?

Wayne stared at the barracks looming above him and felt the headache coming on that came with organizing a search party for the entire island.

Locals would have to be cajoled or flat out bribed into helping. The island would have to be divided into grids and each grid checked and rechecked. The barracks alone presented a huge safety hazard that would no doubt result in a lawsuit if some idiot local tripped and fell through the rotting —

"Dad." Jimmy said. "Over here."

Jimmy's voice was a little too loud and when he met his son's eyes, he knew it was bad.

Wayne hustled over to the opposite side of the stone well, where Jimmy had been hauling on another goddamn cigarette, and found his son staring down at a stone sticking out of the ground near the front steps of the barracks.

What the hell?

Wayne's eyes flicked from his son to the rock protruding out of the ground, as he still tried to make sense of what he was looking at.

He edged closer, and bent down to examine the object, as Jimmy backed away. For Wayne it was like staring at one of those weird images at the mall. Those ones where if you looked at the image long enough, your eyes would finally relax and the image hidden in the design would reveal itself. Well, Wayne never saw shit in those tricky things, but he damn sure recognized a face when he saw it.

Marcus Avernus stared straight up at the sky from the unbroken ground. There wasn't a shovel mark or a grain of disturbed earth anywhere near the man's head. It was as if he had been planted there years ago and now, the face of Marcus Avernus had finally broken the surface, and bloomed.

The grey skin of the man's face had been torn to shreds, and hung from his skull in leathery flaps. His mouth was frozen, opened wide as if caught in a yawn, or a scream, exposing a maw filled with broken teeth. His eyes were gone, gouged out, and from the dark sockets sprouted thin black tendrils of what looked like seaweed, but more muscular, like they were the tentacles of jellyfish.

"What the fuck?" Jimmy asked from a distance. "I mean, seriously, Dad. What the actual *fuck?*"

Wayne stared in horrible fascination at the unbroken earth, the way Marcus' head looked like it had been pushed up through the ground from beneath. The pressure in his chest returned and squeezed his heart. He felt as though his lungs were flattened allowing him only sips of air.

Behind him Jimmy was rattling off question after question, but his voice became a droning white noise in his ears. Nothing Wayne saw made sense, and he damn sure had no answers.

CHAPTER

FOURTEEN

The alarm rang and as soon as Sarah opened her eyes, she felt the knot in her stomach tighten. She swatted at the alarm clock and silenced some happy pop song she didn't recognize.

Daylight leaked around the edges of the blackout blinds they had installed in the bedroom so Dan could sleep during the day before his night shifts. She lay there, wrapped in her blankets, a cold pit of dread forming in her stomach and debated.

But what was there to debate? She had seen the stack of overdue bills and the apocalyptic state of their bank account. She needed to return to work, otherwise there was a real chance of them losing the house.

They had reduced the price twice in the last year, and even took out a small loan to renovate the downstairs bathroom, in an attempt to update their house that was permanently stuck in the eighties, with its pink and green wallpaper, and silver tube and glass furniture.

The house had been Dan's aunt's. At first Sarah hadn't wanted to redecorate out of respect, but over time it became less and less of a priority until it wasn't a priority at all.

When Sean got sick, they mortgaged the house for as much as the bank would allow to cover the medical costs. At the time Sarah and Dan would have given up pieces of their own bodies to ensure Sean got a full recovery. But when he died, it was all for naught.

The expensive treatments from faraway places like Sweden and India had failed, which left Sarah and Dan with a dead son and a mountain of debt.

Their realtor, a chubby, bottle-blonde woman in her forties who never seemed to stop smiling had explained that the area was in a 'downturn' and the only properties that were moving were way below what they were asking.

The consensus was clear. They were stuck. They needed money to, not get out of debt, that seemed impossible, but to stay afloat. To be allowed to remain in their shitty '80's house in a neighbourhood that was slowly being vacated and boarded up, Sarah needed to go back to work. Dan was already working all the overtime he could and sometimes she would find him asleep at the kitchen table still dressed in his uniform.

She needed to go. She needed to get up, get dressed and go to work. She was lucky that Glen, her boss at the local library, had held the position for her. He was a nice older man in his sixties, that had a soft spot for bow ties and peanut brittle, but at the end of the day he couldn't hold the position forever.

Sarah swept back the comforter and swung her legs over the side. The house was silent and cold.

Dan had taken a shift guarding the perimeter of some movie shoot downtown and Rose was already at school. There was no excuse.

Still, she thought of calling Glen and explaining that she still wasn't ready. He would sigh sadly, and say things like *'you poor dear'* to make her feel less guilty about leaving him short, again. But it would be all right. He would console her, and she would apologize and then she would do it all over again tomorrow. Or in a week.

Her green eyes flicked from her cell phone on the bedside table to the dress she had picked out last night that hung from her closet door.

She thought of spending another lonely day in the house, looking for things to do that would take her mind away from thinking about Sean. She figured if she was going to clean out the pantry again, or rearrange the garage one more time or other similar, mindless work all day she might as well get paid for it. Besides, she didn't think she could handle the look on Dan's face when she told him she just couldn't do it today. She couldn't go back to work. *Again.*

She knew he wouldn't scream or yell, or even look disappointed. He would nod and slide his hand over hers and pull her into a hug. He would murmur something that sounded like, *'it's gonna be all right.'* But it wasn't true.

Without giving herself a chance to talk herself out of it, she pushed up off the bed and shuffled into the bathroom. An hour later she was showered and dressed in the light blue dress she had picked out the night before.

The dress hung from her thin frame, at least a couple sizes too big now. She had lost weight over the last year. Apparently, watching your son slowly die in front of your eyes, and then having to plan his funeral really put a stranglehold on one's appetite.

She curled her shoulder-length red hair while she listened to Chris Stapleton sing about Tennessee whiskey, and even applied a light dusting of makeup.

When she was finished, she barely recognized herself in the mirror. Her cheekbones were high and looked razor sharp under her skin, but she was still pretty. Even with the hollows around her eyes. She leaned in close to her own reflection and saw the flicker of a smile touch the corner of her mouth.

Not bad. She thought. *Not bad at all.*

She stepped into the hallway and saw Sean's bedroom door. Instantly the knot tightened in her stomach and all the guilt came rushing back. She was betraying him. She was abandoning him and worse, she was forgetting him.

"No." She said aloud. *"No."*

She shook her head and powered forward. As she descended the stairs to the first floor the queasy feeling persisted, tugging her backward, desperate for her to spend one more day in bed. Just one. One more day drifting over the floorboards of their home. Haunting the place even more than her dead son.

She had to go.

Now.

Instead of making herself a travel mug of coffee or packing herself a lunch like she had planned, she decided not to risk it, not to give the house another chance to talk her out of it, and strode right past the kitchen to the front hall closet. She grabbed her coat and pushed straight through the front door.

FIFTEEN

Glen was shocked when Sarah pushed through the front doors. He actually stopped in mid stride, his expression tentative, as if he didn't quite believe what he saw.

Sarah raised a hand in a casual wave as she crossed the floor to the service desk. The smile grew and bloomed across the old man's face, and he hurried through the hinged half-door arms wide.

"Oh, my goodness." Glen cooed. "So glad to see you!"

Glen was a few inches shorter than Sarah, especially in her heels, but he wrapped his arms around her and squeezed the air from her lungs in a powerful hug.

"Damn good to see you." He said as he released her. "Damn fine. And you look amazing!"

"Thanks." Sarah replied, when she could breathe again. "I appreciate holding my spot, Glen."

Glen made a sour face like he had just bit into a

lemon and waved her away, as if the very suggestion of replacing her was never on his mind.

"This is your position, Sarah." He whispered, his voice was nearly always library volume, Sarah thought, except for the night she and the rest of the library staff got him to sing Karaoke at Big Texas on his birthday last year. That night he gave Gloria Gaynor a run for her money with his warbling rendition of *'I Will Survive.'*

"Well, thank you, Glen. I appreciate it."

"And you picked a good day to return as well. I brought in some of those doughnuts from the vegan place on St Paul Street. They're in the back, there's coffee too, well, you know where everything is."

Sarah nodded. She did. She hadn't been gone that long.

"Sorry." An elderly woman's voice rose from behind Sarah. "Excuse me?"

Glen nodded and squeezed Sarah's arm. He dropped her a wink and then turned his smile to the elderly woman shuffling from foot to foot.

"Can you show me where the restrooms are?" The old woman asked.

"Of course, dear." Glen replied and offered his arm.

Sarah slipped behind the service desk and through the Staff Only door.

The staff room was empty and she was grateful. She really didn't want to get into a welcome back tour of hugs and smiles and delicate questions about her grief and her resulting crippling depression. At least not today.

She passed on the box of designer doughnuts and the last dregs of the coffee pot, as her stomach still churned with nervous energy.

With her coat hung on the rack and purse secured in her tiny metal locker she took a deep breath.

You're fine. This was the right thing to do.

Her heart was almost bouncing in her chest. Her breathing rising to match the rhythm. The walls wobbled for a second and her knees turned to water.

Breathe...breathe...

Sarah clawed at the clasp on the tiny locker and pulled her purse free. Inside she found her little orange prescription bottle and twisted off the top.

You already took your pill for today...

"Shut up." She hissed, and dry swallowed another little yellow angel. She closed her eyes and leaned against the wall of lockers until the Valium slid down her throat. Until the walls regained their solidity. Until her blurry vision refocused itself.

Slowly, her breathing returned to normal as she focused and drew in slow, even breaths, held it for a beat, before she pushed them out just as slow.

She once again closed and locked the locker and headed back out to the service desk where she found a loaded cart of returned books, ready for the shelves.

THE LIBRARY WAS WARM, and the wheels of her returns cart quietly squeaked as she rolled, and for a while she didn't think of anything except the books on her cart.

The dull, calming effect of the Valium had spread through her limbs in a slow warm wave.

College and high school students dotted the long research tables in tiny groups, huddled over thick textbooks, while gray haired retirees sat in the comfortable club chairs as they read their morning newspaper.

Sarah felt her chest loosen and as she pushed her little cart through the narrow stacks, she took a deep cleansing breath for the first time in what seemed like forever.

She felt a dreamy smile spread across her lips.

God, she missed the library.

The glossy dust jackets and the slightly musty smell of the books. Even the weight of each work was soothing to her. She missed putting together the little displays of new releases or tables featuring local authors.

As Sarah passed, and pushed her cart toward the non-fiction section of the library, a group of school kids flooded into the children's area. Their muffled voices, a low grumble of half-whispers and gasps as they took in the towering stacks of books and colourful displays.

The kids rushed to the shelves, and their stubby fingers flipped through the spines. They grabbed books by the armfuls and carried them back to the centre of the room where they dropped into beanbag chairs, or set up shop at one of the little tables built especially for them. All the while their harried teacher, a young blonde woman with a pinched expression, tried to keep her eyes on each one of her little charges as some disappeared deeper into the stacks.

The children's area was the thing she missed the most. Sitting in the old wooden rocking chair Glen had refurbished and stained himself. Having the kids sit in a circle around her as she read *Charlotte's Web* or a classic by *Dr Seuss*. She missed watching their eyes grow wide as they got into the story. The delight and fear on their faces as their beloved characters ran head-first into danger and came out the other side, victorious.

But she wasn't ready for that. Not yet. Let Glen or Muriel, one of the other part-time librarians, handle that chore for now.

For now, she was happy just being back. Out of the house and away from Sean's bedroom and the pictures on the walls of his smiling face, his little t-shirts, everything that reminded her of him. Every scuff on the baseboards. Every drawing of his on the fridge that she and Dan had silently refused to throw away. Every beautiful memory that drove a stake through her heart.

Sarah found the right stack and hefted the heavy tome entitled *Astrophysics So Far* by S. Wilson. The book was as heavy as a newborn, and she carried it in the crook of her arm as she crept halfway down the row looking for its home.

She slotted the book next to the author's equally dense work, *Botany So Far,* when she heard the noise.

It wasn't so much a sound, but a feeling. A fishhook in the brain that tugged her head to the left.

CHAPTER

SIXTEEN

At the end of the row stood a little girl in a pink t-shirt with frilly sleeves beneath a pair of denim overalls. Her tiny pink shoes poked out from the wide cuffs.

In the dim light of the fluorescents that hung above the stacks, Sarah couldn't make out much of the girl's face. Her features were a white smear shrouded in shadow, beneath a mop of curly dark hair.

Sarah smiled and shifted her attention back to the stacks and straightened a few errant titles that had gotten pushed too far back on the shelf. When she was finished, she cut a glance to her left and found that the kid hadn't moved. And she was staring at her.

Sarah felt stupid for ignoring her and slowly stepped closer, a big, safe smile on her face. Maybe she was lost. Or needed some help.

"You okay, honey?"

The child still hadn't moved, and she had started to officially creep Sarah out.

Curls of jet-black hair spilled across the kid's face like ink, hiding her left eye. The visible eye was a beautiful blue-grey that sparked in the weak light.

"Come home." The kid whispered.

Sarah wasn't sure she saw the kid's lips move, but she definitely heard her voice, just below a whisper.

Come home...

Sarah forced herself to take another step toward the little girl, her breath smoked in the suddenly frigid air that wreathed her face.

"Come home." The kid repeated, and this time Sarah saw the flinch of the child's cracked lips as she spoke the words. Tiny fissures cracked and snapped, the sound of new ice breaking under the softest pressure.

Sarah stopped in her tracks, a bright fear rooted her in place.

The mysterious child still didn't move. Her beautiful eye, the color of a winter sea, was locked onto her, and pinned Sarah to her spot.

Come home...

Bruises, the color of storm clouds spread across the porcelain skin of the child's arms. The purple hue deepened to a murky green, which darkened to a diseased black as the skin sunk in on itself as the child rotted before her very eyes.

"COME HOME!"

The child screamed. The furious volume of her voice was terrifying and hit Sarah like a slap in the face.

Where was this girl's teacher? Where was Glen? Why wasn't anyone coming?

Boils, pregnant with pus bloomed along the child's neck, which twisted and distorted the gorgeous little girl's features into a grotesque funhouse version of the child.

Sarah felt the scream at the back of her throat, but there was no oxygen. She was desperate to look away, to run away, screaming. But she couldn't move. She was forced to watch as the child disintegrated in front of her.

The little girl reached up with both hands and twined her short fingers into her glossy black hair. With each hand full, she delivered a savage, downward yank with both hands.

A freight train's worth of bile roared up Sarah's throat as the girl's entire scalp was torn in two, accompanied by the sound of ripping leather.

It was finally too much. Sarah's body took over. She moved on autopilot. She stumbled backward, certain she saw something beneath the gore of the girl's face.

She was sure of it.

Under the thin veil of blood and the stringy bits of tissue, there was another face.

She saw the crooked grin, and shape of Dan's chin.

Sean.

She saw her son.

Come home...

Sarah spun and bowled straight into the nervous looking grade school teacher. The collision knocked the bird-like woman into a shelf of chemistry textbooks, and she cried out.

Sarah tripped over her feet and collapsed on all fours to the thin carpet. Instantly, she felt hands on her shoulders, voices growing louder.

"Come home!" The child's voice roared again, louder still. A voice so loud, like the voice of God, Sarah felt as though her head might explode.

Sarah stole a glance back at the child. The diseased, dying girl, dripping with gore. The little girl with Sean's face. With Sean's voice.

Come home...

Someone called her name from far away. She could barely hear it over the screaming. She hauled in a breath and realized that she was the one screaming.

Hands slipped under her arms and she struggled to her knees.

"Sarah!" Glen hissed. *"Sarah, please."*

Glen was crouched in front of her, still holding her shoulders. His face a twist of fear and concern. His Adam's apple bounced wildly up and down atop his yellow bow tie decorated with tiny red dots.

Sarah looked back to the end of the stack where the blonde teacher had knelt down in front of the little girl in the coveralls. The child was crying, and the front of her coveralls were darker than the rest.

The teacher scowled at Sarah as she climbed to her feet and led the weeping child away.

"Can you stand?" Glen whispered, as his eyes searched her pale face.

Sarah nodded and she let Glen help her to her feet. Once there he stayed with her, his gnarled right hand lightly gripping her elbow, in case of another fall.

"Do you want me to call someone? Do you want me to call Dan?" He asked.

Sarah shook her head. Other, less frightened children had crept to the edge of the stack and were staring at her, hoping for a bit more drama.

"I'm okay." She whispered, her voice hoarse, her throat sore. But Glen was already shaking his head, a mixture of concern and fear writ large across his face.

"Oh honey." He told her as gently as he knew how, "You're not. You're not at all okay."

SEVENTEEN

Dan finished early and picked up Rose from school. He loved watching her bounce down the sidewalk from Holy Cross Elementary in her blue plaid skirt and white blouse. A huge smile on her face as she ran from the school like the Devil was chasing her. She had tied her hair into pigtails, and they bounced too.

He envied her.

They had all gone through something terrible. Something life changing, and although Rose was sad, she was able to carry on with her life in a way that mystified Sarah and himself. He had heard all the cliches about how children are resilient and could bounce back from trauma easier than adults, but it didn't help him. Most days he walked around feeling as though he was carrying a backpack full of concrete. Weighed down by grief and he felt guilty about ever feeling happy.

He saw her smile as she ran toward him, a smile

bursting across her face and wanted what she had. He wanted it so badly.

Rose hit the passenger side of the truck with a thump and then wrenched open the door. She tossed her backpack onto the rear seats and before she was even seated, she began speaking in her usual rapid-fire way, "Guess what Jasmine brought to lunch? Guess? Guess, Dad! *It's so gross.*"

Dan pulled away from the curb, careful not to mow down any oblivious eighth graders that ran across the parking lot without looking, eyes glued to their phones.

"Seriously, guess, Dad." She said, again. "You'll never guess."

Rose snatched Dan's cell phone from the cupholder and quickly plugged it into the truck's stereo with an auxiliary cord.

"Also, I got a new song. You're gonna hate it, but maybe not...you never know. You can be cool sometimes."

"Oh, thanks."

A moment later a heavy bass line thrummed from the truck's speakers vibrating the change Dan had left in the centre console.

"A little loud." Dan said.

Rose shrugged and turned the volume down a few degrees.

"So, what did Jason bring to lunch?"

"*Jasmine.*" Rose corrected. "Sardines! Can you believe it?"

"What's wrong with sardines?" He said. "I used to eat them all the time. They're good."

Dan stole a glance at his horrified daughter. She looked as grossed out as if he had told her he had eaten babies as a child.

"I can't even." She said finally. "Tiny little fish? In stinky oil?"

"Don't knock it til you try it."

"It's carnival people food." She said and Dan chuckled. "Food for monsters."

"Rose, come on. Tell me you didn't say that to...whatshername."

"Of course not, but everyone was thinking it."

Their truck turned onto their street and Rose went quiet. Dan followed the kid's gaze out through the windshield and saw what she was looking at: Sarah's pale green civic was parked in the driveway. They both knew her shift at the library wasn't supposed to end for another two hours.

"Mom's home." Rose said, with no enthusiasm.

"Be nice, okay." Dan told her. Rose nodded and sat back in her seat. "I'm serious."

Their eyes met and he saw the mature woman that hid inside his thirteen-year-old daughter.

"I will." She whispered. "Promise."

DAN STEERED the truck into the driveway beside his wife's car and killed the engine.

Rose dragged her backpack out of the truck and jogged up to the front door, and pushed through. Dan could hear Nina Simone playing inside and knew it would be bad.

He straightened the FOR SALE sign on the front yard, stomped on the wet ground to wedge it into place and then let go. The damn thing slumped back to the wonky angle and stayed there.

Fuck it.

Dan thought about ripping the useless thing out of the ground, but instead he scanned the neighbourhood.

It was the middle of the afternoon, but no one was out. He couldn't hear the drone of people mowing their lawns or the smell of meat being grilled on barbecues. It was the first warm day of spring, and the neighbourhood was dead.

The volume of Nina Simone rose as the front door opened. Rose leaned against the doorframe.

"Burgers okay with you?" She asked.

Dan nodded and shuffled inside. Rose held the door and as he shrugged off his coat she gestured upstairs.

"She's up there." She said. "I'll start the barbecue."

Dan grabbed a beer from the fridge and climbed the creaking steps to the second floor.

Nina's deep, soulful voice rose and fell as she sang about wanting a little sugar in her bowl.

At the bedroom door he grabbed the handle and pushed slowly inside as the first song ended and *Sinnerman* slowly began.

Their tiny bedroom was as dark as a tomb. Sarah had pulled down the blackout shades he used during the day.

He used the weak light spilling in from the hallway to find his way to the bed where Sarah lay on her side, a cool damp cloth over her eyes. Wads of scrunched up Kleenex littered the bed and a wineglass stood empty on the bedside table.

Dan told *Alexa* to turn down the volume and she complied. He set his beer down next to her empty wineglass and curled into her back, sliding his arms around her. She leaned into him, and he could feel her body shudder as she wept.

"It's okay." He whispered as she cried. "It's all right."

Sarah didn't talk for a long time.

A LITTLE WHILE later Rose eased open the bedroom door and peered inside. Dan's beer was gone and Sarah was asleep, snoring quietly.

"Dad?" Rose whispered from the door.

"Yeah, baby?"

"Dinner's ready."

"We're coming, honey." Dan told her, and listened to his daughter's light footsteps retreat over the hardwood.

Dan swept Sarah's red hair away from her cheek and kissed it. She stirred and for a moment she even smiled. An exhausted, still a little fuzzy from all the wine, smile. But Dan still counted it as a win.

"I think Rosie made dinner for us."

"What?"

"I know." Dan said. "We better get down there."

Sarah rolled out of Dan's arms until she was flat on her back. She stared at him through the gloom.

The sunshine of her smile evaporated almost instantly, smothered by a storm cloud of worry and doubt. Dan had lived with that face for the last two years. The familiar crease between her eyebrows returned and her mouth formed a thin line. Dan could almost hear the whirring of gears in her head, revving up.

"What are we going to do?" She asked.

"Eat." Dan said. "Come on."

He kissed her again, and she wriggled away, pushing herself up into a sitting position.

"I'm serious, Dan."

"Me too." He said. "I'm starving. And we'll figure it out, okay? You aren't ready to go back. It's okay."

He tried to wrap his arms around her, to pull her in, but she resisted. Her whole body thrummed with anxiety.

"It's not okay, all right? Stop saying that."

"What do you want me to say, Sarah?" Dan replied, careful to keep his tone low and his words soft. He didn't want to fight. He was too tired.

"Agree with me that we're fucked, Dan. You keep saying everything is gonna be all right, and it's not. It's not ever going to be all right, because Sean is never coming back. Ever."

Sarah's eyes sparkled with fresh tears and when he pulled her close, she didn't fight it this time.

"We are fucked. Financially. Emotionally. Properly fucked. Okay? I said it. But we're not beat and we're still together." Dan said. "Sean is gone. He's dead and it kills me every day to know that I'll never see him again. But it doesn't mean we have to die too. We have to go on, Sarah. We have to fight. I'm not done, and I know Rosie isn't done. But we need you with us."

Sarah swiped a face full of tears away with a back-hand and said, "What about the house?"

"Fuck the house." Dan said. "Fuck this pink and green monstrosity. We'll get *whatshername* to lower the price again and then maybe we can get the hell out of this city."

"You wanna move?" Sarah asked. "Where?"

"It doesn't matter, okay." Dan told her. "As long as we're together. That's the deal, right? Together forever."

For the first time in a long time Dan saw a flicker of life behind her eyes. A glimpse of the old fire he fell in love with.

"We can do anything, honey." He said. "As long as we're together."

CHAPTER

EIGHTEEN

It was three days later, a Sunday, and the weather was perfect. The sun was shining and baking the pavement, and Dan could actually believe that summer was on the way.

Sarah sat in their tiny backyard on a lounger with her nose in a new Maeve Binchy book, a glass of iced tea nearby, while Rose transformed the rickety wooden picnic table into an artist's studio.

With no threat of rain, she hauled out her tackle box of pencil crayons and markers, and an oversized drawing pad they had bought her at an art supply store downtown. It was the kind with the thick paper that could hold up against the smears of glue and the weight of glittering stickers she would inevitably apply.

The scene was perfect. The day was perfect, as long as Dan didn't think about Sean.

He sipped his coffee as he sat opposite his daughter, and just watched. He watched her scrutinize the blank canvas. He loved the way her soft, little hand hovered over the pencil crayons. Fingers wriggling as she made a last second decision to grab the sea foam green and not the forest green.

"Good choice." Dan said, and nodded toward the pencil crayon clutched in her fist.

Rose blew a tangle of black hair out of her eyes and said, "It's not as easy as it looks. Mess up the start and the whole thing is wrecked."

"I hear you."

"I'm serious, Dad."

"*I know.*"

Rose gave him the *side-eye* as she tried to decide if he was messing with her. He usually was.

"Hey you two." Sarah said, "Anyone getting hungry?"

Rose shook her head and went back to her sketch.

"I was gonna cut the grass." Dan told her.

"Okay." She said and lifted her book from her chest and went back to reading. "Let me know and I'll get something going."

It had been only three days since Sarah had tried to return to work and failed, but Dan thought she had turned a corner. Occasionally she still moved around the house like she was dragging a piano behind her, and her eyes seemed to be permanently ringed in bruises, but he had hope.

Dan had contacted their realtor and gave her the go-ahead to knock another ten thousand dollars off the price. She suggested twenty and they settled on fifteen. If the house sold, they would be lucky to break even. But Dan knew that right now, what his little family needed was a fresh start. Somewhere new. Somewhere they could make new memories and start again.

He finished the last of his coffee and strolled over to Sarah. She tipped the corner of her book down to peer up at him.

"What?" She asked.

Dan leaned down and delivered a chaste kiss on her lips.

"Gross." Rose muttered from the picnic bench.

Sarah smiled and stared up at him.

"What was that for?"

Dan shook his head, "Nothing. Just like kissing."

"Seriously, Dad?" Rose said.

"Okay. Okay." He told Rose. "I'm going."

Dan groaned as he rose and crossed their tiny yard. He pushed through the man door of the garage and raised the main garage door. The lawnmower rested beneath a row of bikes that had fallen over. He pulled up one after another, shifting them to the left to free the trapped mower buried beneath the pile. First his, then Sarah's. The next belonged to Rose and then finally Sean's.

He knew it would be under there. He knew it, and braced himself, but the sight of the electric blue BMX still took his breath away.

He grabbed the ridged, rubber hand grips and

suddenly he was back, standing in the street in front of his house on a forgotten October Saturday. When the cool breeze had the bite of a coming winter, and the flaming red, and brittle, golden leaves skated across the asphalt.

Sean was so determined to do it all himself. To be big like his sister and ride a *'big-boy-bike'* as he put it. Sarah was so nervous, Dan had to practically hold her in place as Sean pushed away from the curb by himself on his first solo ride. They watched holding each other as their son's bike wobbled wildly as he furiously pedalled, gaining speed.

Rose had called out for him to keep going. To pedal faster. And he did. Thin legs pumping up and down as the bike sped away, the nervous trill of his laughter rising and falling as he swept through the circle at the end of their street and made his way back.

Dan could feel that kid's grin, it was that big. So happy. So proud of himself.

'You see mom? I didn't fall. Not once!'

Sarah had wriggled out of his grip by then and wrapped the little boy in her arms as soon as his feet stepped off the pedals.

He remembered bonfires of dead leaves and s'mores later that night. Sticky faces and fingers smeared with melted marshmallow and chocolate. He remembered carrying Sean upstairs at the end of the night, his thin arms draped around his back, his hair full of wood smoke, his soft breath warming the crook of his neck.

The sound of a car's engine as it swung into the driveway pulled him from his reverie.

Dan dragged a hand over his face to wipe away any stray tears and stepped out of the garage.

A sleek new Mercedes growled to a stop behind his truck and a tall, thin man with a mane of slick brown hair climbed from the driver's seat. He was dressed in a tailored suit that probably cost more than Dan's entire wardrobe. *Twice.*

The man scanned the depleted neighbourhood with an irritated scowl that made Dan think this guy had gotten lost somehow.

He watched as the man fished a fob out of his pocket and tapped a button. The headlights on the luxury car flashed and the horn gave a little chirp as the security system was activated.

Only after the man laid eyes on Dan did his scowl soften, his smile widen. Dan stopped moving as a fist of ice clenched in his guts.

What now? Dan thought. *Was this guy from the bank?*

"Daniel Avernus?" The man asked, as he strode up the drive. "Are you Dan Avernus?"

"That's me." Dan told him.

The man's grin graduated into a full-blown smile, full of large, polished teeth. He offered his hand and Dan shook it. The man's hand was soft, but the shake was firm.

"Good to meet you, Dan." The man said. "I'm Anderson Seville. I was a friend of your father."

Dan held the man's hand in his own and tilted his head as Anderson's words sank in.

"You said *was*, as in, *was a friend of my father?*"

Anderson broke the handshake and dimmed his smile considerably to a wattage just above a grin.

"Is there somewhere we can talk?"

Dan squared up to the other man, everything about his body language screamed go away.

"We can talk right here." Dan said. "This won't take long."

"Right to it." Anderson said with a flash of that practiced smile. "Like your dad."

"Cut the bullshit, okay? Whatever you're selling, I don't want any and I don't care." Dan told him, an edge in his voice now. "What are you doing here?"

"Dan?"

Sarah stood at the end of the driveway, near the garage, her empty iced tea glass in one hand.

"Everything okay?"

"Hello." Anderson said. "You must be Sarah. Nice to meet you. I'm Anderson."

Sarah looked puzzled, but her curiosity drew her closer to the expensively dressed young man.

"I'm sorry, do I know you?" She asked.

"No." Dan said. "Mr. Anderson was —."

"Mr. Seville, actually." Anderson corrected.

"Mr. *Seville* was just leaving."

"Actually." Anderson said, as he took a sidestep away from Dan's scowl and toward Sarah. "I really need to talk to you. I've been looking for you two for a while. You guys aren't easy to find. But I really do need to talk to both of you, Dan. It's about your father's estate and I promise, you're gonna want to hear this."

Sarah caught Dan's eye and with the tiniest of looks he knew he was overruled.

"Of course." Sarah said. "Come on back."

Anderson's eyes flicked to Dan who shrugged and swept a hand toward the backyard.

A FEW MINUTES later Sarah brought out a tray filled with drinks. A glass of Pinot for her and two beers; she handed one to Anderson. He thanked her, glanced at the label and set it down on the table as if it might bite him.

Rose continued to draw, her piece taking shape. She

raised her head only once and smiled at Anderson as he passed. She said hello and went back to her drawing.

Anderson opened his mouth to say something complimentary about the kid's work, but stopped when he saw the child's drawing. His professionally arranged smile withered and died on his face.

The little girl was filling in the jagged rocks she had drawn with black pencil crayon. She stopped when the tip broke, but she was quick with the sharpener, and soon she was shading in the rest of the knife-like protrusions that ringed the tiny island in the centre of the paper.

A piece of land that looked an awful lot like Avernus Island.

"She's constantly drawing." Sarah told him. "Aren't you sweetie?"

Rose gave her mother a courtesy nod, but didn't look up. Eyes laser focused on her work.

Dan led Anderson to the circle of Adirondack chairs that ringed a steel drum the family used for a fire pit, and took a seat. Just far enough away to be out of earshot, but close enough so they still kept an eye on Rose.

Dan smiled as the prissy young man examined the burnt wooden seat flecked with ash. Anderson took a few nominal swats at the chair with a dark hankerchief, but resigned himself to sit. The man actually winced as he squatted and perched himself on the edge of the chair.

Dan hid his smile by taking a sip of beer.

"Everything okay?" Sarah asked.

Anderson nodded and recharged his smile.

"Fine. Thanks."

Once he was settled Dan found the man's eyes.

"If you wanted to tell me my father was dead, you coulda just called. I haven't seen him in fifteen years."

"There's a little bit more to it than that."

"How did he die? If you don't mind." Sarah asked, and then shot a look at Dan to see if she had over-stepped. He shrugged and she turned to Anderson.

"He...it was an accident apparently. A fall. Out on the island."

"That's awful."

"What was he doing out there?" Dan asked.

"What island?" Sarah said.

"Dan's island." Anderson told her. "Avernus Island."

Sarah turned to Dan who was already raising his hands in defense.

"You own an island?" She asked.

"Whoa. Wait. I don't own an island. My family. My *father* owns an island." Dan said. "And it's not what you think. It's all rocks and a crumbling building. It used to be a leper colony for Christ's sake. Not exactly Maui."

Still, Sarah looked hurt to be left out of the conversation.

"I had no idea." Sarah muttered to Anderson. "Of course, Dan never talks about his father."

"I didn't tell you because it didn't matter. It still doesn't matter." Dan said to Sarah. "It's not mine."

"It is now." Anderson said, as he took a tentative sip of his beer, grimaced and set the bottle down again.

"So who are you, anyways?" Dan asked. "An estate lawyer?"

"No." Anderson told him. "Actually, my technical training is in music history."

"*Seriously?*" Sarah said.

"Yeah. I spent four years at Yale studying the history of music but when I graduated, I realized that as far as career paths go, I was pretty limited."

"*Really?*" Dan said sarcastically.

"Yes, Dan." Anderson said. "But those four years taught me more than where Beethoven died."

"Where did he die?" Sarah asked.

"I can't remember." Anderson told her. "But the four years I spent at school taught me what I was good at, and that was getting people what they wanted."

"You lost me." Dan said.

"I tell people that I'm a consultant," Anderson continued. "But really what I do is find things for people. Rich people, usually."

Dan and Sarah shared a glance and then Sarah said, "Yeah. Sorry. Completely lost."

"I met your father a year ago. I was working on a project for the Kaminski brothers. Are you familiar? You heard of them?"

Dan and Sarah looked at Anderson like he was speaking a foreign language.

"What about *Ninjatech*. They made the video game *Monster Factory* and *Dead by Dawn*."

A lightbulb went off for Dan and he said, "Yeah, yeah. Sean plays that one."

CHAPTER

TWENTY

For a moment no one spoke. Dan could feel Sarah's body tense into a fist beside him but there was nothing he could say.

Had.

He used to play that one...

Dan had said enough. He took a swig of beer and then after a beat, Anderson powered forward.

"The Kaminskis hired me to find them an island to purchase. I had a laundry list of things that each prospective island had to have and yours, I mean, your father's island, was my top pick."

"For what? What do they want to do with it?"

"Who knows? Once they told me it was going to be a new west coast headquarters for *Ninjatech*. The next time I saw them, it was going to be a resort."

"A resort?"

"It doesn't matter, Dan." Anderson said. "Whatever they plan to build will have to be approved by the village of Oak Bay, and a whole bunch of other government offices that honestly, hurt my head just thinking about. But that's not our problem."

"Our problem?" Dan asked.

"Yes, Dan." Anderson told him. "We're in this together now."

"Who would want to buy an island that was a former leper colony?" Sarah asked.

"Up until twelve hours ago," Anderson told her, "the Kaminski brothers. But I can't sell it without you, Dan."

"Why me?"

Anderson leaned forward and spoke to Dan as if he were a particularly slow child.

"Because when he died, your father left everything to you. That's why I'm here. It's all yours, Dan. The house on the mainland, his old pick up, and most importantly, the island."

The weight of what Anderson had said took a moment to sink in and he stole a glance at Sarah.

"Did we just become rich?" Dan asked.

"Oh my god..." Sarah couldn't breathe. She kept staring at the fussy young man sitting on the edge of her Adirondack chair unable to stop the smile from spreading across her face.

"What's the island worth?" Dan asked.

"Our asking price is $37 million."

"Holy shit."

"The problem is that the Kaminski brothers are looking at two other properties. With the untimely demise of your father and the subsequent investigation into his death, our deal has been delayed for weeks."

"What investigation? You said he died in a fall. An accident." Dan asked.

"He was apparently alone on the island, and his death did raise some concerns."

"What concerns?"

"Nothing serious, but the Oak Bay Sheriff, Sheriff Roberts, I don't know if you remember him at all, but he's kind of a stickler and he's been pushing to keep the investigation open."

"Why?"

"I don't know." Anderson told him. "He won't talk to me as I'm not family. He won't even talk to Ruth, but he will talk to you."

"Who the hell is Ruth?" Sarah asked.

"She was our housekeeper when I was a kid. I can't believe she's still there." Dan said, and then to Anderson. "What did Ruth say about his death?"

"Ruth told me and the cops the same thing. One night, just before dark your dad went over to the island and never came back. When he didn't return the following day, she called the Sheriff's Office."

Anderson shifted on his perch and said, "I spoke to the deputy, the Sheriff's son, he said the damage to the body suggested a fall, but that's all he would say."

"Fall from where?" Dan asked. "The only thing high enough out there are the barracks, but it doesn't make any sense."

"Honestly Dan, I don't know. That's why I need you to come back with me."

"What? Where?"

"To Oak Bay, Dan. To meet with your father's lawyer and take possession of the estate. Your father and I, stood to make a fortune in this sale, Dan. But we have to act fast."

Anderson pulled out a plain white envelope from the pocket of his suit and set it on the table.

"I need you to fly to Oak Bay and claim your inheritance as soon as possible. In the envelope there's a certified cheque for $5000 to cover airfare, car rental, and whatever else you need to get there."

"This is unbelievable." Dan said, his head spinning.

"I just hope we're not too late. I stalled the Kaminskis all this week while I was trying to find you, but we have to move fast. I need you to make the right decision now, Dan. I need you to come home."

Dan's grin faded as he replayed Anderson's final words.

Come home...

Rose blinked and let go of the black pencil crayon. Her hand ached and her fingers in that hand felt numb and tingly. She stared at her drawing and frowned.

So many jagged black lines and the weird, creepy building with the broken windows. This couldn't be right. She must have not heard him correctly.

Her parents were still talking to the man in the fancy suit and barely noticed as she held up the drawing for her dead brother to see.

Sean stood in the empty field beyond the chainlink fence that bordered their backyard. He was too far away for Rose to clearly see his face, but she could tell he was smiling with that little sly grin of his. She had done well.

He was pleased.

CHAPTER

TWENTY-ONE

The Oak Bay Sheriff's department was housed in a squat concrete building with exactly three windows that overlooked Elm Street. A few battered cruisers, long past their prime, and the Sheriff's Bronco sat parked out front.

Ruth steered Marcus' Ford pickup into one of the three empty spaces for visitors and killed the engine.

Rain had been falling in sheets for hours, battering the roof and windows of the house. As she sat in the pickup the machine gun rattle of the rain did its best to drown out her thoughts. Her thoughts about reversing out of the parking spot and going home. Maybe throwing the damned diary into the fireplace.

Warm orange light spilled out of the Sheriff's Office windows and sometimes someone would pass by. Sooner or later, someone would notice her sitting out here. She either had to go in or go home. *Shit or get off the pot*, as her mother would say.

Margaret Bleekman, the Sheriff's dispatcher pushed through the front doors and extended a transparent umbrella decorated with tiny yellow ducks. She did her best to shield her large frame from the rain as she hustled over the flooded sidewalk to her yellow Jeep Wrangler.

Margaret paused when she recognized Ruth through the windshield. She raised a chubby hand and then continued on, almost diving into the little Jeep.

Shit. No choice now. Ruth thought.

If there was one thing Ruth knew, it was that Margaret would tell Sheriff Roberts she saw her parked in the lot out in the rain. She might even be texting the man now from her vehicle.

Ruth craned her neck to scan the lot of employee parking further down the street, but she couldn't see Margaret's Jeep.

"No choice." She whispered and grabbed the leather-bound diary. She had taken the precaution of sealing it into a *Ziploc* bag to keep it out of the rain, but forgot to bring an umbrella for herself.

No matter.

Ruth clutched the diary to her chest and stepped out into the rain. She shuffled as fast as her arthritic knees and hips would allow and pulled open the front door to the Oak Bay Sheriff's Office.

∽

THE NEXT DAY DAN, Sarah and Rose spent the morning in the stuffy office of Mr. Lawrence Tuttle, the attorney of record for the estate of Marcus Avernus.

His tiny office stank of old books, dust, and some sort of curry dish that lingered in the air, not unpleasantly. He was a small man, barely five foot five, but he made up for it with his weight. To Dan, he reminded him of a boll weevil, and wondered how the spherical man managed to stay upright on his tiny feet.

With a soft voice, Mr. Tuttle offered them coffee and when they declined, he led them to his office at the rear of the building. Smiling at Rose with a set of expensive veneers, he offered her a seat at an empty desk, with a view of the street. Rose smiled and unpacked her drawing pad and a few pencils.

Mr. Tuttle spoke slowly and deliberately explaining the process in its entirety, and then finally, the reading of the will. There were no surprises, except that somewhere down the line Marcus had made Ruth the beneficiary of his life insurance policy.

The ownership of his bank accounts, and the property, including the island, was to be transferred to Dan.

After Dan had signed where he was required and had thanked Mr. Tuttle for all he had done, they moved through the office to collect their daughter, and found that she was gone.

Her backpack was left open and sat beside her chair. Her writing pad was left atop the desk, the beginning of a drawing taking shape. It was a single face, but Dan frowned at the detail.

He lifted the pad and studied the image more closely.

The proportions of the face made Dan think it was a child, but something about the eyes made the subject seem older. The dark eyes were drawn in such a way they seemed to withhold something. A secret.

A threat.

"Found her." Sarah announced from somewhere behind Dan. When Dan turned and found Sarah leading Rose by the hand, he caught her staring at her drawing pad.

"She was in the bathroom." Sarah told him.

"Everything okay, honey?" Dan asked her.

Rose nodded and then broke away from her mother, and snatched the drawing pad from Dan.

"Hey." Dan said. "I didn't mean to snoop. It's good though, Rosie. Super creepy."

Rose glared at Dan, but he ignored her, shifting his attention to Sarah.

"Ready to go?"

They said goodbye to Mr. Tuttle and piled into their rented SUV. Rose sat in the back, and clutched her backpack, which contained her drawing pad, close to her chest.

As Dan pulled away from the curb, he kept an eye on Rose. Her eyes were pinned to a spot on the sidewalk across the street. Her lips moved as she whispered something he couldn't hear, to someone standing on the street, that he couldn't see.

～

It was surprising how easily the memory of his hometown came back. As he drove through the little village, crossing Killaly Street and then Clarence, the names of the streets brought back a flood of childhood memories. Some of them good. Most of them.

"When was the last time you were here?" Sarah asked, studying the storefronts along the the Main Street.

"I just turned eighteen." He told her. "Right after my mom died."

Sarah studied his face as he drove and slipped her hand over his thigh. He gave her a smile as he squeezed her hand.

"You doin' okay?" She asked.

Dan nodded and kissed her fingers as the town faded behind them and the houses got farther and farther apart.

"I'm good. You?"

Sarah nodded and actually smiled. He had noticed her breathing had changed. Since Sean got sick it was as if she was always bracing for a blow. Breathing shallow. Always guarded and tense. Now though, with a change of scenery, a new future ahead of them, Sarah had allowed herself to relax, at least a little bit.

The road rumbled down toward the water and soon the Pacific Ocean filled the windshield, rolling and sparkling as it crashed on the hidden shore below.

"What about you, peanut?" Dan asked Rose. "You doin' okay?"

Rose gave her father a thumbs up and asked, "How much farther?"

Dan turned right at the end of the road and then pointed to a clapboard house set high on a hill.

"See the white house up there, with the red shutters?"

Rose leaned against the back of Dan's seat and nodded.

"That's it." He said. "We're here."

CHAPTER

TWENTY-TWO

D an parked in the long driveway behind a shiny new Escalade and his father's old pickup. He switched the engine off and just sat there in his seat.

Sarah unclipped her seatbelt and already had her door opened before she noticed Dan wasn't moving.

"Babe? You okay?"

Dan stared up at the house and then the pickup.

Christ, the pickup was the same. He thought. *Well, of course it was the same, Dad never bought anything new until he had to.*

"Come on, Dad!" Rose cried. "Let's go already!"

Sarah caught his eye and smiled, a real smile, and followed Rose up the driveway to the stone path that lead to the front steps.

Dan slipped out of the truck and headed up the path. He looked up when the screen door creaked and a ghost from his past stood at the top of the stairs.

Ruth stood there waiting, her hands clasped in front of her. Sarah held Rose back at the bottom of the stairs, and allowed Dan to catch up, and head up before them.

He bounded up the stairs and without a word, wrapped the old woman up in his arms. He squeezed her and lifted the old woman right up off her feet forcing a little squeal from Ruth.

"It really is you." Ruth whispered. "You're home."

"It's really me." Dan told her.

When Dan finally set Ruth down, she held him at arm's length, studying him, smiling.

"You look so much like your father." She said. Tears filled her eyes and her face flushed.

"I'm so sorry, Dan."

Dan hugged her again and felt the bones of the woman's back through her thick sweater. She looked older than when he last saw her, which made sense, but he noticed that she had lost weight. Her plump cheeks were gone now, hollowed out and dark smudges ringed her tired eyes.

"I missed you, Ruth." Dan told her.

Ruth pulled him into another hug and held on as tears spilled down her cheeks.

"You got so old." She said, and Dan barked out a laugh.

"Thanks."

"Handsome, I mean. And tall."

"You look exactly the same." Dan said. "Maybe a little grayer, but otherwise, it's like time stood still around here."

Dan caught Ruth's eye spying the two women over his shoulder and broke from her embrace to pull Sarah and Rose closer.

"Sorry, Ruth, this is my wife, Sarah."

"She's so pretty." Ruth said, and then to Sarah herself, "You're so pretty."

"Thank you. It's nice to finally meet you."

"And who's this little angel?" Ruth asked, as she bent low to get a good look at Rose.

"This is Rose." Sarah said.

Ruth smiled down at Rose, who looked up at the old woman from beneath the edge of her white Cherry Pain toque.

"And you're beautiful too. I love your boots, sweetheart."

Rose did a happy little jig in her knee-high pink rubber boots decorated in yellow ducks. Ruth smiled and clapped when Rose was finished. Rose dutifully took a bow.

"Thanks." Rose said. "I like your house. It's right on the water."

"It is." Ruth said. "Do you like the water?"

"Love it." She said, "We used to go to the lake all the time."

Ruth stared at Dan.

"What's this *used to*?" She asked. "If I remember correctly, you were quite the water bug. I could never get you to come in."

"I still like the water, we just haven't been up to the lake in a while is all."

"Well," Ruth said to Rose. "We have a whole ocean here at the house with all sorts of beasties. Maybe later you and me can take a walk on the beach if it's okay with your parents."

"Can we go, Dad? And check it out?" Rose asked.

"In a bit, okay honey." He said and stifled the next fifty questions Rose had with a quick look. "I promise."

The screen door opened behind Ruth and Anderson Seville peeked out looking slightly annoyed.

"You're finally here. Good. I was about to send out a search party. Come on in."

Anderson ducked back inside.

"I take it you've met the weasel?" Ruth whispered to Dan.

Dan nodded.

"A necessary evil for the time being." She said.

"Come on in. I made some cookies just for you, Rose. Do you like oatmeal chocolate chip?"

"They're my favourite."

"Same as your Dad." Ruth said. "That's interesting."

"Oh, I'm very interesting." Rose added, as she grabbed Ruth's hand and nearly pulled her through the front door. "So what kind of sea monsters are in the water? Do you have any pets? How long do you think we can stay? Are there any kids that live around here?"

Sarah nodded to Ruth trying to field Rose's rapid-fire questions. "She has no idea what she's in for."

"I bet she loves it." Dan said. "There haven't been any kids here since I left."

Dan held the door for Sarah, and he stepped inside his boyhood home for the first time in over fifteen years.

A long staircase ran along the right side of the home and at the top, on the narrow landing between floors, stood a man Dan didn't recognize. He was trim and fit and dressed in designer casual clothes. He stood in the corner of the landing and held his cellphone up toward the ceiling as if searching for a signal.

Anderson put a hand on his back and guided him away from the stairs and toward the dining room where another guy Dan didn't recognize sat at the end of the table wearing headphones and stared at a laptop.

"Dan, this is Bryan Kaminski."

Bryan was probably thirty-five, but looked younger thanks to the extra fifty pounds he carried that gave his face a youthful look. A bag of Doritos was open to his right, next to a bottle of *Mountain Dew*.

Bryan pushed the laptop away and dragged his headphones down away from his ears as he stood.

Through the headphones Dan could hear the sounds of agonized digital screams.

"Bryan," Anderson said. "This is Dan and Sarah Avernus."

Bryan wiped off the Doritos dust from his fingers and reached out a chubby hand to Dan.

"Nice to meet you." Bryan said. "Sorry to hear about your dad."

"Thanks." Dan said. "This is my wife, Sarah and my daughter, Rose. Actually, I think she's in the kitchen with Ruth."

"I saw her. Pink boots, cool Cherry Pain toque."

"Yup." Dan said. "That's her."

"Fuck it." The well-dressed man on the stairs hissed as he pounded down to the first floor.

"And that charming gentleman on the stairs," Bryan said, "is my older brother, Terry."

Terry Kaminski pocketed his phone and strode over to meet the new arrivals, hand outstretched.

"Sorry, Terry Kaminski." He said, "This place has the worst cell reception. Ever since we got in my phone hasn't received a single text and then over in the corner I suddenly get a hundred."

"No problem." Dan said.

"When did you guys get in?"

"Just over, what? Three hours ago, now. Anderson picked us up from the airport. I was so sorry to hear about your father. We met only once but he seemed like a decent man."

"Thanks. I appreciate that."

Rose came back from the kitchen with a fistful of cookies.

"Rose. Seriously?" Sarah said.

"Ruth practically forced me to take them." Rose said. "You want one?"

"I do, actually."

Rose handed a cookie to her mother and then turned her attention to the chubby gamer sitting at the table.

"Sarah, can I get you a cup of tea while Dan brings in the bags?" Ruth asked.

"I would love that."

"Can I get one of those?" Terry asked. "And maybe a cookie?"

Ruth waved him back and he followed Sarah and Ruth toward the back of the house while Anderson and Dan went back outside for the luggage.

FOR A WEIRD MOMENT the room was empty except for Rose and Bryan.

"I like your toque." Bryan said finally, a little unsure around children.

"It was my brother Sean's. *Dead by Dawn* was his favorite game."

"Oh. What's Sean playing now?"

"Nothing." Rose said. "He's dead."

Bryan's eyes flicked over to the kid's face, looking for the joke, but didn't find one.

"Yeah, well, sorry to hear that."

"It's okay." Rose told him. "He's still around somewhere."

Bryan blinked and then turned his eyes back to the screen, more than a little unnerved.

"Well, Cherry Pain is super cool. She's probably my favourite character."

"You play *Dead by Dawn*, too?"

"Of course. Can I tell you a secret?"

Rose nodded as she chewed her cookie.

"I designed it."

"You did?"

Bryan nodded, thankful that the conversation moved away from dead siblings and into more comfortable territory.

"You designed *Dead by Dawn?*"

"Yup."

"Any others?"

"Yeah, you know *Monster Factory?*"

"Awesome."

"*Midnight Massacre?*"

"Super cool."

"...and *Jelly Pop*."

"Oh..." Rose said. Her face scrunched up like she stepped on a thumbtack.

"I know. I know." Bryan explained. "Terry thought it was going to be the next *Candy Crush*."

"Dude, it was soooo lame with the unicorns and the—"

"—lollipops, I know."

"But I like the other ones." Rose told him. "Have a cookie."

Bryan accepted and together they munched their cookies while Rose studied the laptop screen split in two. One side was running a complex code while the other displayed what looked like a stripped down third person shooter style video game.

"What are you working on?"

"It's not really ready yet. It doesn't even have a title."

Rose peered at the screen with the rudimentary, almost skeletal graphics of the characters attacking each other.

"What's it about?"

"I can show you. Maybe you can help me with it. Tell me what you think."

"Of course! Oh my God! Yes! I still can't believe you made *Dead by Dawn*."

"But you gotta ask your folks, okay?"

Rose nodded but couldn't take her eyes away from the screen.

"Sean has to see this." She whispered. "He's going to go mental."

Bryan stared at the strange kid hunched over his laptop and then self-consciously, and maybe a little nervously, scanned the little cottage looking for ghosts.

CHAPTER

TWENTY-THREE

With their teas in hand, Ruth and Sarah lead Dan and Anderson up the stairs with the bags.

"You and Sarah can have your father's room." Ruth told Dan. "I put Rose in your old room. I hope that's all right."

Dan shuffled into the large bedroom and set down the suitcases. Sarah was already at the French doors that led to a small balcony that overlooked the cobalt blue Pacific Ocean.

Anderson dropped the bags inside the door and then examined his fingers as if he had handled donkey shit.

"Thanks Anderson."

"I'll see you downstairs, Dan." He said, before he disappeared into the hall.

"If you need anything let me know." Ruth said. "Dinner will be about an hour."

"Can I help with anything?" Sarah asked.

"Thanks, but that Terry fella already paid for the Cafe to bring some pasta over. Should be here soon."

"Cafe Amore?" Dan asked. "It's still there?"

Ruth nodded and said, "Nothing much changes around here, Dan."

"Thanks again, Ruth." Dan said, "For everything."

"You know." She said. "Your father wasn't an easy man to get along with at times. He was stubborn and sometimes said things he didn't mean. I'm not making excuses. I'm not. But he did love you, Dan."

Dan didn't know what to say so he said nothing. He pulled the old woman into another hug and breathed her in.

Rose water.

She even smelled the same.

"Is it all right if I take Rose to the beach?" She asked. "Just a short walk before dinner?"

Sarah looked at Dan already nodding.

"Of course."

"Okay," Ruth said with a smile. "See you in a bit."

Sarah moved to the balcony doors and peered out at the ocean beyond.

"This place is amazing. Why have we never been here before?"

"I left here when I was just a kid." He said. "My dad and I didn't get along after my mother died, so...I don't know. We fought and said some things. Some really horrible and stupid things. I joined the Army, moved around a bunch. I kind of always thought there would be more time."

"Is it weird being back here?"

"You have no idea." Dan said. "Like I'm in the freaking *Twilight Zone*. This place hasn't changed at all."

Sarah turned and faced the king-size bed.

"What about sleeping in your parent's bed?"

"Yeah." Dan said. "That's a hard no. After dinner I'm gonna have to run to town and get us another bed."

"Are you serious?"

"As a heart attack."

"You can sleep in this bed for one night." She said and pulled him close.

"It's gonna be so weird."

Sarah kissed him then. Softly at first and then a little deeper, and Dan actually felt her tongue slip over his.

"Maybe a little weird is what we need."

Dan laughed.

"I think you're weird, weirdo."

Sarah slapped him on the arm and took his hand, dragging him to the door and into the hall.

"I can't believe you called me a weirdo!" She said with mock disgust. "Now you gotta give me the tour."

DAN'S CHILDHOOD bedroom was small with a single bed, a dresser and a writing desk. Faded navy blue wallpaper dotted with compasses, anchors and sea monsters lined the walls.

Dan leaned against the doorframe as Sarah drifted through the tiny room and lifted framed pictures of a smiling Dan as a toddler, a radiant mother and Marcus.

The shot was taken at a beach somewhere with a pristine blue sky in the background. Their skin is bronze, and they are sitting behind each other like Russian dolls. Marcus in the back, with his arms wrapped around Dan's mother, who has her long thin arms coiled around her wriggling, smiling son.

Sarah touched the little boy's face in the photo and her fingertip drew a line in the dust. The boy's grinning lopsided smile was so close to Sean's it was uncanny. She set the photo down and brushed away a stray tear.

"You okay?" Dan asked.

Sarah forced a smile and nodded.

"You looked so much like him."

Dan reached for her, but she shifted away, shaking off the sadness that threatened to root her in place and sap her of her good mood. She smiled at Dan and kept moving, deeper into the bedroom. Dan met her at the window and followed her gaze down to the front yard as an Oak Bay Sheriff's cruiser parked in front of the house.

"Why are the police here?"

DAN AND SARAH joined Anderson and Terry Kaminski at the front window as they watched Sheriff Wayne Roberts and his son Jimmy, slip out of the cruiser and stride up to the front door.

Ruth and Rose, both dressed in their rain slickers and rubber boots, stopped at the edge of the grass.

"What the hell is this?" Anderson hissed.

Dan ignored him and moved to the front door.

"Ruth?" Dan said. "Everything okay?"

Ruth nodded and then turned to Rose. She whispered to his daughter and Dan saw from the disappointed look on her face that their beach walk was cancelled, at least for now.

A moment later the foursome shuffled back toward the house.

Dan stepped out onto the porch and asked,"What's going on, Ruth?"

Anderson was close behind him, and aimed all his questions at Ruth. "Did you know they were coming?"

The two Oak Bay police officers eased their way up onto the porch in front of Dan, and the older officer extended his hand. Both cops ignored Anderson who looked like he might have an aneurysm at any moment.

"You must be Dan. Marcus' boy." Wayne said. "Heard a lot about you."

The Sheriff's shake was solid, and his hand felt rough and hard as old asphalt.

"You look like him." Wayne continued. "He was a good man your dad. I liked him a lot."

"Ruth, why are the police here?" Anderson asked again but Ruth was silent, and wouldn't meet Anderson's eyes.

"Sorry, but we just got here, and I really don't know what's going on." Dan told Wayne. "Is everything all right?"

"Actually, no, Dan." The Sheriff said. "Everything's not all right. Do you mind if we come in?"

CHAPTER
TWENTY-FOUR

"He literally just got here, Wayne." Ruth said, and then to Dan. "I was going to let you settle...at least unpack. Have some dinner."

Wayne cocked an eyebrow and turned to Ruth.

"You didn't tell him?"

"Tell me what?" Dan asked.

Behind him Terry Kaminski watched from the dining room table, where even his brother Bryan looked interested, and had closed his laptop.

"No, *Jesus*, Wayne." Ruth said. "Like I said, I..."

"Why don't you just go ahead with it now...wheels are already in motion, Ruth." The Sheriff told her.

"What wheels? What the hell is going on?" Anderson hissed. "Why are the police here?"

Ruth finally looked toward the young man and stared at the thin vein that pulsed in the centre of his forehead.

"Ruth...?" Dan asked.

"I think we should all go sit down." Ruth said finally. "I don't wanna do this standing up in the foyer."

Everyone followed Ruth and slowly assembled around the dining room table. Ruth shuffled ahead and caught Sarah's eye, pulling her farther along toward the kitchen.

"I know we just met, and I hope I'm not overstepping," Ruth said, "but the police are here to talk about Marcus, and some other, less pleasant things that might not be suitable for little ears. I don't want the first conversation she hears to be about the dead."

Sarah studied the old woman's face. She could see that she was worried and even a little scared.

"There's a beautiful beach at the end of the pier." Ruth told Sarah. "I don't think this will take long."

Sarah nodded and gripped Rose's hand.

"You ready for the beach?"

"I've *been* ready." Rose told her.

"All right then."

Sarah smiled at Rose and squeezed Dan's arm as she and Rose slipped through the crowd and disappeared out the front door.

With the women gone Anderson was up and buzzing in Ruth's ear, furious.

"What the fuck is happening, Ruth?" Anderson hissed. "Are you serious right now with this? Did you know this was happening?"

"Sit down, Anderson." Ruth told him in a quiet, but firm voice. "And stay quiet."

The two glared at each other until Anderson finally

blinked. He felt Dan and the rest of the men staring at them. The Sheriff looked like he was ready to beat him with a rubber hose.

With Anderson distracted, Ruth stepped past him and fetched her purse from the pegboard by the front door and returned with the leather-bound diary still inside the clear plastic freezer bag.

With everyone seated around her table Ruth took her place in the remaining seat and removed the diary from the plastic bag.

She set it down reverently in front of her. No one said a word.

Ruth stared at the little book as if it might bite her and then, after a moment, she looked up and met Dan's eyes.

"The night Marcus left...I haven't been well, and I haven't been completely honest. To anyone. He didn't just leave out of nowhere. We had an argument."

"About what?" Dan asked.

"I had to go to Wayne, Sheriff Roberts, and make sure I told him, cause otherwise I don't...I don't trust myself to..."

Ruth seemed to crumple then, her shoulders rolled forward, and she looked somehow older. Tears welled up in the old woman's eyes.

"I never thought the day would come that someone would want to buy the island. That they would actually come here and dig it up. Build something on it. I figured…I figured it was…safe."

"*Safe?*" Anderson asked. "Safe from what?"

Ruth ignored him and pushed the battered leather diary toward the centre of the table.

"This is my great-grandmother's diary." Ruth said as she stared at Dan. "Our families are connected, Dan. They have worked together for generations and I'm pretty sure my great-grandmother had an affair with your great-grandfather, Captain Daniel Avernus. And being so close to him she…she became more than his lover. She was his friend. His confidante."

"Why are the police here, Ruth?" Anderson asked, an edge to his voice.

"Just let her finish." Jimmy Roberts said. Anderson shot the deputy a glare, but slumped back in his chair looking sullen.

"I'm getting there." Ruth told him. "Please. This isn't easy for me. I've read this diary a hundred times and never have I breathed a word of it to anyone. *Ever*. I loved your father. He was my best friend. After you left, we were here all alone. Together. And this town is all I've ever known."

Everyone around the table waited in silence as Ruth swiped at a stray tear, took a few deep breaths, and then continued.

"Everyone knows that between 1908 and 1924 the army barracks on Avernus Island was used as a leper colony." Ruth said. "Dan, your great-grandfather was paid by the government for the use of the land and the existing structures to treat those poor souls in isolation. To give them a place of their own. Once the initiative began, Captain Avernus would pick up his passengers from the ports of California and all the way up the coast, and transport them out to the island. It was supposed to be a place where the infected could live out their days in isolation, and relative comfort. Captain Avernus was given money to feed and clothe them, and to even repair the barracks to make it livable for the people, for the families that were to live there. But your great-grandfather had a different idea."

CHAPTER

TWENTY-FIVE

Since being diagnosed the woman and her daughter had spent their last days in the crumbling Oceania hotel. The nuns from the local convent made the rounds at breakfast and again at night and brought stew and loaves of day-old bread.

Those that wanted the bland, lukewarm stew had to venture out across to the back lot of the hotel where an army tent was erected to keep the good sisters out of the rain and snow.

The woman and her daughter shared their cramped little room with another two women who were both much older and further along in their disease. Soon, both of the older women were found stiff in their beds, curled on their sides like dead leaves.

Two days after the deaths of their roommates the woman and her daughter were given the news. Their ship had arrived to take them to a temporary colony off the coast. The nuns they spoke to told them about a comfortable place for them to live until treatment could be arranged. A place with open sky and miles of beach.

The woman had seen too many of her friends and family taken by the disease to hold out hope for a cure, but she thought her daughter would enjoy living so close to the shore.

Later that day large trucks covered in canvas arrived and they were herded inside. The woman clutched at her daughter, pulling her close as more and more of the sick were forced into the back of the truck. Soon the two women could barely move.

The woman counted fifteen people shoulder to shoulder in the back of the truck including her and her daughter. She squeezed her little girl so tight against her side she hoped that she would somehow absorb her daughter. Shield her from all of this.

The madness of the disease they called leprosy had spread across her clear, perfect skin like a voracious weed, sprouting bulges and bumps. Leaving the skin that remained, dry and cracked as a desert floor. As her fellow passengers jostled for position, the scarf she wore slipped from her head. She adjusted it quickly out of habit, and rewrapped the thin veil around her head.

At the port there was a brief respite as the truck ground to a halt with a squeal of brakes and the back tailgate was lowered. She could smell the sea and tang of fish.

As she and her daughter climbed down from the bed

of the truck, they saw seagulls wheeling high in the sky, as they cried out to each other. Tied to the dock was the biggest ship the woman had ever seen, *The Springfield*.

Men waited on the pier. The men wore rags tied around their faces and gripped rifles in their hands. They barked orders as they directed their new passengers up the gang plank, across the deck, and down a ladder into the hold.

A heavyset man with square shoulders and a massive black beard that ended halfway down his chest looked on. This man, she knew from the way all the other men deferred to him, must be the captain of the ship, Captain Avernus. He watched from a distance as they shuffled past. A look of disgust twisting his features.

Soon they were climbing a ladder down into a gloomy darkness lit only by a small lantern. The woman went first, followed by her daughter. Immediately she noticed that the hold didn't have a proper ceiling. Only a wide, heavy hatch. The hatch, she saw, was open to the sky through three-inch squares in the lattice.

The second thing she noticed was that the hold was empty. There were no seats. No beds. Just matted drifts of sodden hay that covered the floor.

The passengers that still had their wits about them, grumbled and swore as they pulled the lantern from where it hung on a nail, and explored the hold that stunk like an animal pen. Some screamed and began to climb back up the ladder, before the men pointed rifles down into their faces and forced them back.

Soon after the hatch was secured and locked.

THE MASSIVE SHIP tilted left and right in the waves, and freezing cold water splashed through the holes in the hatch above.

The screams of indignation and fury soon transformed into the moans of the dying. They were given no food and were forced to collect the rainwater as it fell. Most soaking their cleanest pieces of clothing and wringing the freshwater into their swollen mouths.

The woman and her child huddled together for warmth, and stole the coats of the dead to use as blankets.

Time stretched out, every second more painful than the last. Still, she held her daughter to her, shielding her from the splashes of frigid water and the smell of shit and vomit and blood that sloshed through the hold. The woman wriggled her toes and felt nothing. She squeezed her daughter, felt her heartbeat through her thin flesh and prayed for them to make it to the island; where others like themselves had created a safe space to live, and eventually to die with some modicum of dignity.

Through the holes in the ceiling the woman noticed that the sky had lightened from a boiling black, smothered with storm clouds, to a dove grey. Watery sunlight spilled through the ceiling, and she noticed that more than half of the people in the hold had died during the night.

They lay low in the hold. She watched as the filthy tide swept back and forth, and splashed over their open mouths and half lidded eyes. The dead had been stripped of most of their clothing which exposed their distorted, ravaged skin.

And then they were stopped.

The boat rocked back and forth in the shallow water.

The hatch was raised and she saw the captain stare down into the hold, a rag held over his mouth and nose.

The captain whispered something to one of his sailors who held a lantern, something she couldn't hear, and then a different sailor with a rifle strapped across his back, descended down the ladder into the hold.

At the bottom he swung his rifle around until it was facing the huddled mass of passengers. The woman could see that his rifle was affixed with a long blade, a bayonet.

The sailor found her eyes in the gloom. He had a rag over his face, but she could tell by his eyes and his thin frame he wasn't much older than her daughter. Barely a man.

"You." He hissed. "Get up the ladder. Now."

The woman struggled to her feet. Her joints frozen in place from the days of inactivity. Once vertical, she helped her daughter to stand, and they shuffled toward the bottom of the ladder.

"You lot." The boy cried to the rest of the group. "Everyone up and against the far wall."

Those that could, began climbing to their feet, using the wall of the hold for balance.

The woman stole a glance over her shoulder as some

people lying on the floor, amid the swill of blood and vomit, hadn't moved at the boy's command.

"I said, *up.*" The sailor repeated. "I ain't telling you again."

More passengers struggled to their feet, their tattered clothes dripping with filth as they shuffled to the ladder.

"Last warning." The boy sailor said, as the rifle shook in his hands. The edge of the bayonet threw sparks in the weak light.

The woman was nearly halfway up the ladder now, with her daughter in front, when she heard the groan issued from below.

Her head twisted and she saw the boy plunge his bayonet into an old woman who had ignored his commands and remained lying flat on her back.

The blade entered her chest above her heart and the old lady barely flinched. Which was worse, thought the woman, than crying out. The woman heard the blade scrape across bone as it pulled a soft moan from the elderly woman. Her final breath was a curl of smoke in the freezing gloom of the hold.

TWENTY-SIX

"I told ya." The boy squealed, fresh tears shining on his cheeks. "I warned ya. Didn't I?"

The boy moved to the next passenger lying curled on his side, facing the wall of the hold. Without another useless warning, he stabbed the man between the shoulder blades, and the hold filled with the sound of his blade ringing off the dead man's spine.

The woman turned away and helped her daughter over the edge onto the main deck. The captain glared at her from a distance and she realized that her daughter's head scarf had fallen away.

Rifle barrels poked her in the back as sailors led them to a small skiff that would be lowered to the water.

The woman clutched at her daughter and drew in deep cleansing breaths for the first time since setting foot on the *Springfield*. She helped her daughter step into the small rowboat and take her seat. Once the remaining passengers were assembled, the woman counted six including herself and her daughter. Captain Avernus stepped into the bow and the boat was gently lowered into the water.

A few moments later, as their rowboat cleared the bow of the *Springfield,* the woman got her first glance of Avernus Island.

A dark place bristling with jagged black rocks. She saw no tell-tale signs of life. No gray curls of smoke rising from the island. There were no people on the shore to greet them.

ONCE ON THE island their small group was ordered off the boat and onto the beach. They followed a sailor through a twisting path through massive columns of rock until they passed beneath a towering arch of stone into a large, empty courtyard. The crumbling remains of the Army barracks loomed above them.

She had been told by the good sisters that there would be a place for them here. A place where they could be warm and cared for. A place with medicine and food.

There was only a strange black column of volcanic glass protruding from the center of the courtyard. As they drew closer to the strange formation, the woman realized it was hollow resembling a bizarre well. She couldn't see the bottom, but she could hear the weak drone of flies rising from the depths.

The sailors shouted for their group to stop and then prodded the lepers into forming a single line, shoulder to shoulder.

The woman held her daughter close, she could once again feel the little girl's heartbeat. Feel it rising, faster and faster.

Her daughter knew the truth as well as she did. This island was not a new beginning. Not an oasis, but a grave.

A light rain began to fall but the woman barely felt it. Her fellow passengers shuffled into place, their soiled shrouds plastered to their mottled, ruined faces.

The captain stepped in line with the four sailors who had made the trip.

"Is this all of them?" Captain Avernus asked his first mate.

"Aye, Captain."

The captain then turned his attention to the terrified lepers, his dark eyes swept over each one, shivering in the icy rain.

"Then may God have mercy on your souls."

And with that the captain nodded to his first mate who signaled the rest of the sailors.

"Turn and face the barracks!" A sailor ordered.

Moans and whimpers erupted from the four other remaining passengers, but each turned and complied with the order.

The woman leaned down close to her daughter and squeezed her tight.

"You there!" Screamed a voice she recognized, it was the boy sailor from the hold. "You. Woman. Stand straight."

But the woman ignored him, instead bent closer to her daughter's ear, and whispered.

"Run!"

Her daughter shook her head, as she twisted her head around to face her.

"Oy!" The sailor continued. "You listening? Your ears haven't falled off have they?"

"Forget it, Charlie." The captain said, "Just get on with it."

"I'll be right behind you." The woman whispered. *"Now go!"*

The woman gave her daughter a little push and the child stumbled forward, closer to the well as the captain yelled, "Fire!"

Bullets punched through the brittle chests of lepers and they toppled to the ground in a jumble of limbs.

The child who had fallen on all fours, screamed for her mother, lying on her side in the muck. One side of her face a bloody ruin, left by a sailor's bullet that had torn through the back of her head.

"Mama!"

The child ran and dropped to her mother's side, cradling her ruined head.

The captain twisted toward the sound, annoyed, and pointed at the filthy child as it spun in the mud and took off running for the looming barracks.

"Goddamn it! Go get it!"

Two sailors rushed after the child, their feet pounding through the sodden ground, as their rifles swung in their grip.

The remaining two donned leather gloves and began the process of lifting the bodies of the dead lepers and dumping them over the edge of the massive well.

Captain Avernus stood close to the edge of the well, as he enjoyed watching this bit. The well was very deep. He remembered once lowering a lantern as far as the rope would allow, and still not finding the bottom.

The sailors moved quickly, scooping up the dead and dying and heaving them over the side. Once every so often a damned soul would scream on the way down. The captain quite enjoyed that. It was his favourite scenario. He shot a glance at the two sailors who had chased the little girl into the barracks and wished he had captured her alive.

The child ran blindly into the barracks smashing through the warped doors and into a wide foyer. She looked for a place to hide, fresh tears burning her eyes.

Footsteps slammed through the mud nearby and the girl bolted for the far side of the room. She reached for the doorknob as the same door exploded inward. The girl skidded on the wet uneven floor and fell to her knees.

The girl's filthy shroud that covered her face slipped away and the sailors flinched and swore aloud at seeing the child's true face.

The girl's long black hair had fallen out in handfuls revealing a knobby white skull. Her face was distorted with boils and bulges that twisted her features into a monstrosity.

Her hot breath boiled in the air around her head as she changed course, moving on all fours, back the way she had come across the ruined room.

The two sailors moved in and aimed their rifles.

With no exit, the girl stared back at her hunters. Her hideous expression transformed from fear to rage. A scream grew in her chest as she rose to her feet. She would not be killed on her knees. She dreamed of clawing them to shreds and spreading her disease to them. To all of them for what they did to her mother. For what they were doing to her.

She opened her mouth and a roar fueled by pain and sorrow and fury exploded from her tiny body as she surged forward, toward the sailors.

The rifle butt smashed into the back of her head with a sickening crack, and she dropped to the floor in a crumpled heap.

Captain Avernus stood above her, a rifle clutched in his hands. He prodded the little girl with the barrel of his rifle and saw that her slender back still rose and fell. She was still breathing. Still alive. A smile spread across his lips. *This trip wasn't a total loss.* He thought.

He caught the eye of the sailors standing in a loose circle.

"Pick it up." He told them. "I want to hear her fall."

CHAPTER

TWENTY-SEVEN

OAK BAY, OREGON

When Ruth was finished you could have heard a pin drop in the cramped little dining room. For a few moments no one spoke, and the only sound was the wind buffeting against the house, rattling the little decorative spoons and the framed pictures on the wall. That was until Anderson said, "You gotta be fucking kidding me..."

Ruth spun in her chair and glared at the smug young man, "What? It's the truth."

"Why? Because some chick wrote it down in a dream journal a hundred years ago?"

"Hey, how 'bout a little respect?" Sheriff Wayne Roberts barked and fixed his own glare on Anderson.

"No, wait." Anderson said, "Are you serious, Ruth? Dead lepers?"

"Murdered lepers..." Jimmy said. "Hundreds of them."

So far Dan hadn't said a word. He looked stunned like someone had kicked him in the gut. Ruth reached across the table and gripped his hand.

"I'm so sorry, Dan."

"Wait, wait, wait. I take it no one has been out there to verify this, right?" Terry said.

Wayne eyed the newcomer in the fancy clothes carefully designed to look like he belonged in the woods, or or a nature hike eating granola.

"That's right." Wayne told him. "Not yet."

The Kaminski brothers stared at each other, then at the Sheriff.

"So we gotta go out there." Terry said. "Check it out."

Bryan shot a withering look at his brother, but Terry ignored it.

"Jimmy and I are going out there tomorrow, first light, to see if we can get into that well and either confirm or deny...what Ruth told us."

"Christ, Ruth. How could you not tell me this before?" Anderson whined.

"Maybe because she figured you would make it go away." Jimmy said, taking a real dislike to the perfectly coiffed man.

"Why would I do that?"

"Really?" Wayne spat. "I heard all I need to know about you, Mr. Seville. If one of the founding fathers of Oak Bay is revealed to be a greedy, homicidal maniac with a mass grave of defenseless bullet ridden lepers, I'm figuring the sale might be affected. We're simple out here in the sticks, but we ain't stupid."

Dan just sat there as he tried to catch his breath and thought of a way out of this mess. A way forward. How would he tell Sarah? How could he tell her that there was nothing here for them? No money. No new start. No future. All that was gone. In an instant.

All gone.

Wayne stared at him, waiting, as if he had been asked a question. All Dan could hear was the blood rushing in his ears.

"Dan?"

"Sorry, what?"

"I said, we're going over in the morning." Wayne said. "Are you okay with us handling it, or—"

"If you guys are going over there, I want to go too. It is my island now." Dan said.

"I think we all should go." Terry agreed.

Wayne eyed Terry suspiciously.

"I don't think that's a good idea, *Mister?*"

"Kaminski." Terry told him. "Call me Terry."

"Well, Terry. I don't think it's a good idea. The island and the barracks could be very dangerous, and I wouldn't..."

"Can I be blunt, Sheriff?" Terry said, cutting off the older man.

"Go ahead."

"My brother and I want to buy the island. We are still in."

Bryan looked shocked, but Terry ignored it.

"We are still in, but I won't lie to you. Ruth, Dan, this is all quite a shock. But going forward my brother and I need to be in on everything that happens regarding this situation, or we will pull out right now."

Dan stared at Terry and knew he couldn't say no. Without the Kaminskis he might as well just go home right now. There was nothing for him here except a drafty old house that he couldn't sell and didn't want to live in.

"Okay, Terry." Dan said. "I'm good with that."

Terry nodded and still ignored his brother burning a hole in the side of his head with his glare.

"As of right now this whole production falls under the umbrella of helping out an old friend." Wayne said. "We don't know what it is we're gonna find out there. To that end, I'm not blind to the implications of something like this becoming public knowledge. Small town rumours spread faster than a fart in an elevator, so anybody wants to come out and help, fine. We could use it, considering it's just me and Jimmy. But if there is any evidence of what Ruth said, I'm gonna seal the area until the proper experts and authorities can be called in to examine the site. Those poor people deserve that at least."

Terry and Bryan stared right back at the Sheriff, their expressions flat.

"So come if you want, but if anyone tries to interfere with this investigation, they'll have to answer to me. Do I make myself clear?"

TWENTY-EIGHT

The front screen door creaked open, and a dripping wet Sarah and Rose stepped into the mud room and stomped the rain from their boots.

"Til tomorrow then." Wayne said and rose to leave with Jimmy, with Dan close behind.

A moment later Anderson was up and heading toward the Kaminskis like a cruise missile. Terry held up a hand and it had the desired effect: Anderson stopped in his tracks like a well-trained dog.

"Can you warm up the car, Anderson?" Terry said. It wasn't a question. "We're gonna head back to the hotel."

Anderson nodded and the brothers retreated from him, drifting deeper into a private corner, their heads bent together in a whispered conversation.

"Gonna watch the rest of my show upstairs, Mom." Rose said, as she bounded up the stairs and out of sight.

"Okay honey."

Ruth was left sitting looking alone at the dining room table. She twisted her hands together on the surface of the table, wringing them out as tears threatened to spill down her cheeks.

Sarah slid into a chair close to her. The younger woman slid her hand over Ruth's and squeezed.

"How much did you hear?" Ruth asked.

Sarah smiled.

"Enough." She told her. "As soon as we got our boots on it started to rain. Kinda killed the beach walk."

"And Rose?"

Sarah shook her head.

"She had her headphones on. She didn't hear a thing."

Ruth nodded in appreciation, glad for small mercies.

"I'm so sorry, Sarah." She whispered. "I may have ruined everything but..."

"You did what you had to."

"I never thought Marcus would race out to the island...I was just trying to protect him. Protect the family and the town."

Sarah pulled the old woman into a hug, and she could feel Ruth shaking in her arms.

"I should've burned the damn thing years ago." She whispered into Sarah's shoulder.

When Sarah finally leaned away from Ruth, she saw that the woman's eyes were ringed in black.

"You want some tea?" Sarah asked, but Ruth waved it away.

"It'll keep me up." She said. "I do have whiskey."

Sarah smiled, "Even better."

TERRY AND BRYAN KAMINSKI watched Anderson grab his raincoat and push through the front doors into the rain.

"So, what does this mean?" Bryan asked.

"It means that tomorrow just got more interesting." Terry told him.

"No, I mean. What does it mean for the island? We aren't seriously considering going through with the sale. *Are we?*"

Terry looked at his younger brother as if he had grown two heads.

"What are you talking about? You want to bail?"

"Murdered lepers, Terry? We've run into PR nightmares before but how the fuck do you spin this?"

Terry shook his head. He almost felt sorry for his baby brother."You never did have a head for business."

"What? There's a well full of dead lepers on the island. Killed. Murdered. Lepers, Terry."

"Maybe. Maybe not. Either way we get the island. And if there are bodies in that well, they can cut that asking price in half."

"Why would we still want it? You know what kind of nightmare that would be?"

"The *Netflix* special alone will be worth the publicity." Terry said.

"*Netflix?*"

"Sure, or *HBO, Hulu*, whatever. We relocate the

bodies we give them a proper burial. We look like heroes as we generate truckloads of money for the surrounding towns. Who gives a fuck about the Avernus legacy. In a year from now, Kaminski is the only name these yokels are gonna remember."

DAN FOLLOWED the two lawmen onto the porch and Wayne asked Jimmy to start the car and warm it up a touch. Jimmy took the keys and hustled through the cold rain to the cruiser.

"Sheriff, can I have a word?"

"I thought you might." Wayne said. "Sure am really sorry about your father."

"I appreciate that." Dan said. "I wanted to ask you about the circumstances. I mean, how did he die, exactly? Anderson said it was an accident."

Wayne nodded.

"The medical examiner ruled that he died from injuries related to a fall."

Dan looked puzzled.

"But what does that mean? Fall from what?"

"The army barracks out there are three stories high, the theory is that he was up on the roof for some reason and...either jumped or fell."

"Why the hell would he be up on the barracks?"

"I don't know, Dan. I wish I did." Wayne said. "I liked your dad. I thought he was a solid guy, but we all have our demons. If this leper story turns out to be true, the

Avernus name is gonna take a beating. We both know that."

Dan nodded, his breath puffing out in the cold air.

"And the injuries?"

"Are consistent with a fall. The way we found him, he was plugged in the ground almost up to his neck."

"What?"

"The way we figured it, the ground was all soft from all the rain, and when he fell, he, well, sunk into the mud. And when the ground dried up...He broke several big bones including his neck. Whatever happened it was fast. I'm sorry, Dan."

"And when you went out there...did you see the well?"

"It looked like he cracked it open, knocked a hole into the cap the size of a silver dollar, but I couldn't see into the bottom. This selling of your family's island is a big deal. Not just for him but for the whole town and the surrounding towns. He was under a lot of pressure. I've seen people crack under less."

"So, you think it may be suicide?"

"I don't know. Out of respect for your father we agreed to give him the benefit of the doubt and called it an accident and that's how it's gonna stay."

Dan nodded.

"'Night, Dan." Wayne said, and gave Dan a solid clap on the shoulder. "See you tomorrow."

TWENTY-NINE

Later, when Sarah eased into Rose's bedroom to tuck her in, she thought her daughter would be wide awake, and fight to stay up for just one more episode. Just one more game. But when Sarah found her, she was sitting up in bed, her iPad and headphones abandoned on the bedside table. Her head was turned toward the far, dark corner of the room.

"Rose?"

Rose's head whipped around and for a second she stared at her mother as if she didn't quite recognize her. Her eyes were wide and her face was pale.

Sarah slipped onto the edge of the bed and pulled the little girl into a hug, rubbing her back.

"Oh, honey, what's the matter?"

"Is it true?"

Her voice trembled, frayed at the edges.

"Is what true?" Sarah asked, holding the girl's shining cheeks in her palms.

"Are you going to the island to find the people who got sick?"

Damn it. Sarah thought.

"Honey, you weren't supposed to hear those stories, but there's no one on the island anymore. I promise."

But Rose was already shaking her head. "No. There are. Sean told me. He's there too."

"Rose, I'm sorry if something we said downstairs scared you, but I'm telling you the truth. There's nothing to worry about, and your brother..."

"But what about the people?"

"Those people that were left on that island, that happened a long time ago. Over a hundred years ago."

"They want you to go there, Mom." She said, "You and Dad. And me. Sean says we all have to."

Every time Sarah heard his name it was another cut across her heart. She winced and bore down on Rose, gripping her biceps to hold her still.

"Listen to me, Rose." She told her. "Sean is dead."

"I know, but he's not. He's here. Here with me."

Sarah could feel the tears that burned in the back of her eyes and choked her throat.

"Please don't go to the island." Rose begged her. "Don't listen. Don't go. Something bad is there. It's been waiting, Mom. Please."

"Rose please. Listen to me. Your brother is dead. Okay? He is. And I miss him every day and that will never change. But this island, this trip tomorrow. This could mean a new start for us. For you, for me, and Dad."

Tears slid over Rose's cheeks as she stared up at her.

"We have to do this." Sarah said. "You'll see. Okay? Everything will be fine. I promise. Our new life begins tomorrow, baby."

Sarah squeezed her again and she could feel the girl go limp in her arms. The fight and the fear had bled away.

With Rose in position, Sarah pulled up the heavy blankets until they were touching her chin.

"Ruth has got chocolate chip pancakes planned for tomorrow, all right?"

Rose nodded and forced a smile.

"I'll leave the hall light on, okay, and if you get scared your dad and I are right across the hall."

Sarah dropped a kiss on her cheek and then tiptoed toward the door.

Rose watched her mother leave and listened to the bedroom door creak as it was eased closed. A strip of warm light that leaked in from the hall was enough. She could still see her brother watching from the corner.

He stood perfectly still. His pale face veiled in shadow, barely visible, his blue eyes were tiny sparks in the gloom. A puddle of filthy water reflected a sliver of moonlight pooled around his bare feet.

As she held his gaze, unable to look away, she heard a single word in her mind, less a sound, but more like the feeling of a word. A seed of thought left to bloom in the dark.

Home

CHAPTER

THIRTY

Dan's eyes opened in the dark and he was instantly wide awake. It was still dark outside, but he was filled with a nervous, anxious energy. He needed to get up. Now.

He left Sarah quietly snoring in the bed beside him and padded down the hall to the stairs, where every floorboard he stepped on creaked underfoot.

Halfway down the stairs he saw the soft light coming from the kitchen. Ruth sat alone at the small table, a mug of tea cooling in front of her.

The clock on the kitchen microwave read: 3:37 AM.

"Couldn't sleep?" She whispered.

Dan shook his head and slipped into a chair opposite hers. Ruth's wrinkled face creased into a smile, and her soft hand slipped over his.

"I'm so glad you're here, Dan."

Dan nodded and said, "Did he...ever..."

"Ask about you?" Ruth said, as a smile broke over her

face. "Of course. We got internet hooked up just to watch your kid die on Facebook."

Dan searched her eyes, but they weren't Ruth's eyes anymore. They were darker. Brown, or maybe even black.

He tried to pull his hand away, but her grip was like iron, crushing his hand in hers. Still, she smiled as the delicate bones in his hand cracked and snapped like kindling.

"Did you get our thoughts and prayers, Dan."

She finally let go of his hand and Dan reeled backward. He fell off the chair and landed hard on the kitchen floor. He cradled his shattered hand, as tiny shards pushed against the inside of his flesh. Bile roared up his throat as black spots swarmed across his vision.

He heard Ruth stand as the chair she sat in scraped across the linoleum. Dan knew her heavy steps weren't hers anymore, they were someone else's. Someone who stunk of the sea. Brackish water flooded over the kitchen floor, soaking Dan where he lay.

"You don't write, you don't call." Marcus Avernus hissed. "But you're home now. Where you belong."

Dan stared up at his father's pale face hanging in leathery tatters, at the ruined, black pits of his eyes.

"Home."

Dan jerked awake covered in sweat. His head slammed into the headboard and Sarah gasped beside him, startled.

"Dan?" She mumbled, still asleep. *"S'okay?"*

Dan scanned the bedroom and the blinked against the watery sunlight that streamed through the French doors. He sat up and gripped his right hand with his left. The bones were still intact. He could feel his heart returning to normal. He was okay.

"Dan?"

"Yeah." He told her. "I'm good."

AFTER A SHOWER he dressed and he made his way down the stairs following the smell of chocolate to find Ruth pulling a tray of oatmeal chocolate chip muffins from the oven. He felt himself pause at the doorway as the memory of his nightmare crept back in.

"You okay, Dan?" She asked, a smile curling her lips. "Sleep well?"

"Not great, actually."

"Well, that's to be expected." She told him. "Coffee is ready, and these just need a minute to cool."

She seemed normal, at least to Dan, but he flinched when she touched his shoulder as she passed.

RUTH ANSWERED the knock at the front door and found Deputy Jimmy Roberts filling the doorway. He looked about as good as Dan felt. Washed out, and dark around the eyes.

"Morning, Ruth."

"Come on in." She told him. "You want some coffee? Or a muffin. I know how you like chocolate chip."

The younger man shook his head and seemed to grimace at the very mention of food.

"Nah." He said. "Maybe later. Dad's bringing the boat around, down to the pier. Got some of the high angle climbing gear we need loaded. Can you give me a hand, Dan?"

"Sure."

Dan dumped the last of his coffee in the sink and grabbed his coat from the peg by the door.

Dan followed the kid down the steps of the front porch to where the cruiser was parked down closer to the water.

Jimmy unlocked the tailgate and dropped it.

"When's your dad supposed to get here?" Dan asked.

Jimmy didn't answer. He just dragged more bags of kit and tools toward the edge of the tailgate.

The kid looked sick. And if he would've told Dan he had the flu, he might have bought it. Jimmy's eyes were ringed with dark patches the colour of old bruises and his skin was waxy and sweaty at the hairline.

Movement on the water caused both men to stare. About two hundred yards out a cabin cruiser was slowly motoring toward them, the drone of its engine getting louder.

When Dan looked back at Jimmy, the kid didn't look sick. He looked scared.

"You all right, Jimmy?"

Jimmy shifted until he was staring at Dan. His face was set. He was deciding something, that was clear.

"I gotta tell you something, okay?" He said finally.

"All right."

Jimmy dropped the kit bags in the dirt, and leaned against the tailgate, and fished for his deck of smokes.

"Dad, he told me to shake it off and don't go shooting my mouth off, but hell..."

"What?"

But Jimmy wasn't done talking to himself, psyching himself up.

"I don't give a shit about that Anderson fella, I think he's kind of an asshole, if I'm being honest. And the other two...don't know them from a hole in the ground. But you, and your family. Ruth. Your dad. You're from here. And I liked your dad. I did."

The cabin cruiser was getting closer, the engine growing louder. Soon they would need to get down to the dock and help Wayne secure it to the pier.

"What is it, Jimmy?"

"We told you that your dad's death was an accident."

"Yeah." Dan said. "A fall."

Jimmy nodded, draw a deep pull of nicotine into his lungs, struggling with how to move forward.

"So, you're saying it wasn't a fall?"

The deputy stared at him. The boat behind him cut its engine.

"Jimmy, are you saying he didn't die of a fall? That there was something else?"

"Your father...When we found him...Nearly every

bone in his goddamn body was broken. If he fell, it looked like he fell out of a goddamn airplane, not off some rickety three story building out on that island."

"How is that possible?"

"It was like...something pulled him into the ground."

"Why are you telling me this?"

"I'm telling you we went out there to find your dad and we did...but since then..."

"What?"

"The place don't feel right, okay. Not like it used to. Hell, we used to go out there as kids. Bonfires and girls, drinking, smoking weed...teenager shit. The place was creepy...but it was...*fun*."

"The story, maybe...the story about the lepers." Dan offered. "It's pretty fucked up. Maybe, I don't know..."

"I ain't sleepin', Dan. And don't get me wrong, this is a quiet town, but I seen my share of dead bodies and car accidents and mangled bits. But after bein' on that island, it's like a stink that's clung to me. Following me."

"What do you think happened to my father?"

Jimmy waved and Dan saw that Wayne was closer to the pier than he thought.

"I don't know. But what I do know, and if you repeat this, I'll just deny it. There ain't no fucking way he died from a fall."

Jimmy pitched his cigarette into the stones of the pathway and jogged toward the pier.

"Come on." Jimmy said, "Daylight's wasting."

THIRTY-ONE

Sarah crept to Rose's bedroom door and eased the door open. Rose still lay in bed, facing the window, her headphones over her ears, her eyes fixed to her tablet.

When Sarah eased onto the edge of the mattress Rose jumped and dragged her headphones down.

"Hey, good morning." Sarah said and swept her daughter's hair from her face. "You sleep okay?"

Rose stared at her mother. It was a hard stare and she was using her serious face. The face normally reserved to convey outrage against an early bedtime or god forbid, less screen time. Her green eyes were open wide, and her tiny mouth was a hard line.

"What?" Sarah asked.

"Are you going to the island?"

Sarah nodded. "Of course." she said, "I told you last night."

"But you can't."

"Why?"

"You just...*please, Mom.*"

Sarah pulled her daughter in for a hug, but Rose shimmied away.

"Really?"

"You just have to listen to me, Mom."

"Rosie, I know you're scared of a new place and something has spooked you, but this...this island, this place...this is a big part of our new life. We have to move on and move forward, do you understand?"

"Mom, please." Rose said, her knees pulled up to her chest and her arms wrapped around them. "I don't want you to go."

Sarah reached out and cupped her daughter's cheek.

"We'll be back before you know it, okay? I promise. Now, come downstairs, okay? Ruth made some chocolate chip muffins."

"I'm not hungry." Rose told her and slid beneath the covers.

"Rose." Sarah said as she stood and headed for the door. "Come on, Rose."

"I'm not hungry."

And with that Rose flipped the covers over her head and flopped down onto the mattress.

"All right, honey."

Sarah eased the door closed and took one last look at the mound of blankets on the bed.

"Love you, Rosie."

After Jimmy and Dan transferred the climbing equipment from the cruiser to Robert's cabin cruiser, *Gypsy,* everyone waited in the kitchen eating muffins and drinking cup after cup of Ruth's strong, dark coffee.

Ruth asked about Rosie, and Sarah told her she just wanted to hang out in her bed for the morning. Ruth looked worried, but Sarah assured her that she was fine and that she would wander down when she got hungry. If not, Sarah would blast her out of bed when they got back. All was good.

About an hour later when Anderson and the Kaminski brothers arrived, Jimmy, Wayne, Dan, and Sarah were bundled up, ready to go, and waiting on the porch.

Wayne was the first to move down the steps and stride to the group of three men before their car doors slammed closed.

"You guys look ready to go." Anderson said. "Everyone excited?"

Dan eyed the darkening sky. The daylight that started off so promising was slowly being smothered by a tide of slow-moving clouds the colour of old bruises.

"Looks like weather is moving in." Wayne said. "Best get moving."

The Kaminskis fell in line behind Wayne and Terry said, "Lead the way, Sheriff."

As Terry, Bryan, and Wayne headed down the path to

the waiting boat, Dan snagged Anderson's coat, holding him back.

"Yes, Dan?" Anderson said, and Dan noticed that the man's usual smarminess had not returned. No doubt, his pupils looked about as wide as dinner plates. Whatever he had taken had definitely mellowed him out.

"Everything okay?" Dan asked, nodding toward the Kaminskis. "We good?"

"They're still here." Anderson told him. "So that's a plus."

Sarah and Jimmy passed the two of them on the path and Sarah tossed an inquisitive look at Dan over her shoulder.

"So, the deal is still on?"

"I wasn't exactly privy to their family conversations, Dan, I'm just the hired help, but Terry mentioned something about Dana Miner this morning at breakfast."

"Who's Dana Miner?"

"She's a big producer at *HBO*."

"What does that mean, Anderson?"

"It means, Danny boy, that Terry is hedging his bets. No lepers in the well, he wins. We find lepers, he spins the tragedy into a *HBO* documentary."

"Where he's the hero. And my family...is *not*."

Anderson nodded.

"Sorry, Dan." He said. "Silver lining, you'll still get your money. You just might want to be gone after you do."

"What about Ruth? This is her home."

Anderson eyed the house looming behind him and

saw the old woman standing in the front window, looking over them.

"That will be up to Ruth, I guess."

Dan looked sick.

"You never know." Anderson said, as he made his way down the path. "Cheer up. The whole leper killer diary could be bullshit."

THIRTY-TWO

Bryan didn't feel well. He hadn't slept well, and he barely touched his poppyseed bagel at breakfast in the hotel.

He had talked to Terry all night about the island, trying in vain to convince him that this was a bad idea. A really fucking bad idea, up there with *Jelly Pop*. It was a big gamble at best. But he should have known that trying to derail Terry Kaminski once he was set in motion was all but impossible.

Lepers? Were they actually considering this? From a guy that doused his hands with sanitizer every time he shook hands.

For Bryan, this was all too much.

And now, underfed and cranky from the four hours of fitful sleep, he was on a boat. A boat in the ocean that bounced and dropped over every wave as if it was determined to toss him out of his hard plastic seat and into the drink. He needed to get up. To move.

He grabbed onto Terry's shoulder and stood.

"What are you doing?" Terry asked annoyed. "We're almost there."

"I just need some air."

"Just sit down, Bryan."

"Relax. I'll be right back."

"Bryan, sit down." Terry said. "Now."

"Hey Terry? *Fuck off.*"

And with that Bryan shuffled past his older brother and slipped through the rear door that opened to the stern deck.

He twisted the doorknob and the boat bounced again and jostled him to his right. His knees buckled and he nearly fell. He straightened and found his balance and did not look back. He didn't need to see his brother's eyes on him. He could feel them.

Bryan slipped through the doorway and stood with his back against the wall of the cabin.

Yep, he thought, as soon as he was outside in the freezing spray. *This is much worse.*

The cruiser rose and fell, and he needed to hold on, or he would've been on his ass in under a minute, soaking wet on the slippery deck.

The Sheriff or whoever the hell was driving cut the wheel hard to the right and moving parallel to the island. Which gave Bryan a view of the rocky nightmare as they passed.

Last year, when Terry suggested they buy an island, he had laughed it off. They grew up crammed into a two bedroom apartment that was either way too cold in the winter or way too hot in the summer. As kids they survived on food stamps and welfare, they didn't buy islands.

But here they were.

Bryan would've been happier sitting in his New York apartment watching zombie movies on TV and developing his games in peace. A simple life.

He didn't want to be here, and no matter how this turned out today, he was leaving. Fuck this. This was Terry's deal and if he wanted to do it, he and that sycophant, Anderson, could handle it. Bryan just wanted to go home.

"You all right?"

The voice out of nowhere startled him and his feet skidded on the rubber deck. Bryan turned to his left and saw the deputy Jimmy standing there staring at him.

"You looked a little green in the cabin." Jimmy said. "Just wanted to make sure you're okay."

"I'm not really good with boats." Bryan said.

"So, you wanna buy an island?"

Bryan shook his head, and forced a smile.

"It's my brother's idea."

"Gotcha." Jimmy said. "So you're okay?"

Bryan nodded, "Yeah. Thanks."

"All right then." Jimmy said. "Shouldn't be long. Almost there."

Jimmy headed back into the cabin and Bryan went back to studying the rocky coastline. The jagged rocks jutted out of the rough soil all along the coastline like a crown of thorns. They kinda reminded him of the iron throne in *Game of Thrones*, but that's where the fun stopped.

They had been to the island once before, illegally, before they contacted Marcus Avernus and had done a bit of exploring.

Terry kept going on and on about how *fucking cool* everything was, but Bryan couldn't help but notice that nothing grew on the island. There were no birds and no wildlife to speak of. The only trees on the island were withered gray things that curled up out of the soil like skeletal fists. No leaves. No green. Just black rock and stone.

Bryan felt the *Gypsy's* engine power down as the captain guided them toward the little beach where they would land.

A piece of cloth or a dirty plastic bag was caught in one of the weird trees near the coast. It fluttered in the wind like a ruined flag and given the island's history, Bryan thought it was fitting.

Until the flag moved.

It wasn't caught in the branches of the tree. It was wrapped around something (someone) else. Something standing in front of the thin tree. Bryan watched, frozen in place as the face beneath the shroud turned to follow him as he drifted past.

It wasn't a rag or a bit of garbage. It was a shroud.

Someone was watching. Waiting...

A hand clapped over his shoulder and Bryan yelped.

Terry nearly burst out laughing.

"What the fuck is wrong with you?"

Bryan's wild eyes bounced from his brother to the coast, but the *Gypsy* had drifted too far, and his view of the person wearing the shroud and the withered tree were now blocked.

"There was someone up there."

"Where?" Terry asked, his smile fading. "Are you serious? Are you sure?"

Was he?

Bryan watched his brother scan the coast and then meet his gaze.

"Are you fucking with me?" Terry asked. "Did you really see someone?"

"I think so." Bryan told him. "I don't know."

"What did they look like? Was it kids?"

Terry studied his brother's face as Jimmy the deputy rounded the corner onto the stern deck.

"You ready boys?" Jimmy said. "We're here."

CHAPTER

THIRTY-THREE

R uth sat at the kitchen table sipping Earl Grey tea and struggled through the New York Times crossword. Who the hell knew what professional hockey defencemen grew up in St Catharines, Ontario? She opened the browser on her phone and thought about cheating and *Googling* the answer when she spied the clock on the microwave. It read: 9:51 AM

She had forgotten all about Rose.

It had been so long since kids ran the floorboards that the little girl sleeping upstairs slipped her mind.

She had hoped that she would emerge on her own and they could do something together. It didn't matter what as long as it didn't entail moving too fast. Her knees were not what they used to be.

Ruth thought they could bake some cinnamon rolls to go with the roast beef dinner she had planned for tonight when everyone returned.

She peered up at the ceiling and listened. She tried to

187

remember if she had heard any movement when she was doing the breakfast dishes earlier. Or even a toilet flush.

She couldn't remember, but that wasn't exactly evidence. She couldn't remember what she had for supper the night before.

She would just let her be. Ruth was still a stranger and all. They had just met the other day. Let the child come to you, Ruth told herself. It's fine.

Ruth went back to her crossword puzzle and read the same clue about the Canadian hockey player and slammed down her pencil.

Well, this is ridiculous. Ruth thought. *That kid is gonna sleep the whole day away.*

She drummed her fingers on the table a few times and checked the clock again: 9:53 AM.

"That's enough." She said and hauled herself out of her chair.

On the second floor she edged slowly to Rose's door and knocked gently.

She waited but there was no response.

Slowly, Ruth eased the door opened and saw that Rose was still under the covers. A small mound high up on the mattress near the headboard. She stepped into the room and heard the muffled sound of a conversation. Was she watching TV under there?

Ruth had seen the child toting around one of those tablet *thingys*. Maybe that was it.

"Rose?" Ruth whispered. "Rose, I was just wondering if you'd want some breakfast."

Nothing.

No response. No movement from the mound of blankets.

"Rose, honey?" Ruth whispered. "You awake?"

Ruth poked the mound of blankets and felt only more blankets.

"Rose?" She asked, a little more firmly. No more whispering.

Ruth gripped the edge of the top cover and pulled it down about halfway. And there was nobody there. Just the stupid tablet playing a Japanese cartoon. Even her headphones were left behind. Ruth's heart dropped in her chest and she scanned the tiny room.

"Rose?"

Thunder rumbled somewhere above the house and shook the window glass.

"Rose?" Ruth said, her voice quavering a little. "Come on out now."

THIRTY-FOUR

AVERNUS ISLAND

"Hold on, folks."

Wayne cut the power to the *Gypsy* and drove the bow up onto the beach as close as he could get to dry land. When the boat stopped it sank a little in the sand and then tipped ever so gently to the right.

Jimmy left the bridge and after grabbing the tow rope, leapt over the side onto the wet sand.

"We'll need to push off when we leave, but it's the best we can do." Wayne told the rest of the crew. "Come on out to the bow and Jimmy will help you get down."

Terry shuffled past Wayne followed by Bryan and Anderson. Sarah waited her turn, her head on Dan's shoulder.

"You okay?" Dan whispered.

Sarah nodded and stared out through the windows of the cruiser, studying the rocky beach.

"This place looks like a fortress." Sarah said.

"That was the idea, I think." Dan told her. "Kept unwanted guests away."

Sarah turned to Dan and examined his face in the gloom.

"Did it keep you away?"

Dan smiled. "Course not."

One by one everyone made the jump from the boat to the shore. Jimmy moored the boat to a large outcropping of rock and then climbed back onto the deck and helped Dan unload the gear.

Everyone was given something to carry, even Anderson, who looked exquisitely uncomfortable carrying a greasy canvas bag of tools.

Bryan and Terry toted hard plastic cases, Sarah carried a big cooler bag full of snacks and drinks and a coil of orange climbing rope, while Jimmy and Dan carried the mini-generator for the winch.

With everything covered, Wayne lit a cigarette and waved for them all to follow him.

"It's colder here than on the mainland." Sarah said, her breath steaming in the air.

"Storm is moving in." Wayne told her, as he peered at the sky.

"Thought the weather was supposed to be clear?"

"Since when is weather an exact science? That storm isn't going away. I say we do what we came to and get back to the mainland ASAP."

The group moved silently through the rock forest in a tight single file as the path through the rocks became more and more narrow. Sarah caught herself staring up at the peaks above her as she shuffled behind the old Sheriff dazzled that a place like this existed at all. No grass, no weeds even. Just jagged daggers of black rock, and those weird, twisted trees.

Nothing grew here.

The whole island felt dead.

THE GROUP FOLLOWED Wayne's back and the twisting trail of his smoke through the stone maze until they emerged beneath the massive archway.

Sarah had no words. She shuffled into the watery sunlight of the courtyard and took everything in. The shiny black well, the crumbling barracks looming beyond. It was amazing.

Dan and Jimmy stepped past her, as they grunted with the effort, and set the mini-generator down near the base of the well.

Sarah joined him and stared at the scarred concrete capstone.

"Well, there it is." Dan said. "What do you think?"

"Who would build a well this big?"

"No one built it." Wayne told her. "And it's not a well, at least not in the ordinary sense. It's made of volcanic rock. I don't think the barracks ever used it for water."

"Then what the hell is it?" Anderson asked.

"I've heard of these things...I googled it." Bryan told

them. "Thermal tubes caused by eruptions in the ocean floor."

"So, what's it doing here, Mr. Wizard?" Terry asked.

Bryan shot his brother a withering glance and opened his case, checking his equipment.

The rest of the group moved to the edge of the well and inspected the tiny hole. Terry was the first to aim a flashlight into the gap.

He squinted, leaning over the capstone to get close.

"I can't see anything." He said finally. "Stinks though."

Thunder rumbled above and everyone looked to the darkening sky.

"Looks like you boys better get a move on." Wayne said.

"No time like the present." Anderson said and to the surprise of them all, actually pulled a sledgehammer from the canvas sack and stepped to the capstone.

"You know how to use one of those?" Jimmy asked him.

"Put myself through school working construction jobs with my Uncle."

"See, that surprises me." Jimmy said. "It actually brings you up a few notches."

"Well, that's me, underpromise and overdeliver, James."

"It's Jimmy."

"*Whatever.*"

Anderson swung the hammer like a pro and the

resulting *gong* reverberated around the courtyard and the surrounding buildings like a pinball.

Dan leaned in and inspected the spot where Anderson struck. There was barely a scratch. This was gonna take longer than they thought.

THIRTY-FIVE

Rose was crouched in the dark. The voices were gone now. She didn't know for how long exactly, but Sean had told her to wait. So she did.

She had moved rolls of paper towels and a bucket of cleaning products out of the way to make room for her to crouch inside the small space. A cubby that stank of bleach and sour water.

Her back was starting to hurt from being bent over like she was, and her throat felt raw, and it hurt to swallow.

Finally, the tiny door inches from her face creaked open and her brother peered inside.

He said nothing, which was annoying, and he would answer none of her questions either. He just drifted away.

Rose crawled out of the cabinet and stood up. There was no one on the boat. At least, no one she could see.

Her jeans were wet, and the cuffs of her coat, but other-wise she was all right. She took long deep breaths and tried to clear the chemical taste out of her mouth.

She listened again for any voices and then crept up the stairs to the main deck.

The ship rocked beneath her and the wind bit into her cheeks, but the deck was clear.

Nervously, she scanned the shore and the black jagged rocks that exploded out of the dark beach. They looked like knife points.

Sean waited on the beach. He stood as still as a rock on the shore. Waiting.

When their eyes met, Sean smiled and gestured for his sister to follow him. She shook her head and his smile evaporated. He lowered his hand and turned toward a gap between two rocks and disappeared.

Scared, Rose debated her next move. If her parents found out she had stowed away on the boat without them knowing she would definitely be in trouble. But she had come here for a good reason, and that, she thought, would make up for it.

Finally, she jumped down from the boat onto the shore. The distance to the ground was a lot farther than she thought and she fell forward onto the shore. The sharp pebbles of the beach cut into her palms, but she brushed them off and followed her dead brother into the dark.

～

Above them the sky darkened considerably. The black clouds festered in the grey sky spreading like an infection, threaded with streaks of lightning.

Dan swung the sledgehammer at the capstone and a chunk the size of a toaster fell away, disappearing into the maw of the well. Pieces of the cover fell away faster now, but the cover was built to last. Four inches thick of concrete reinforced with metal bars didn't give up without a fight.

Jimmy crept up to the damaged capstone and shined his light down into the hole.

"Goddamn."

"What?" Anderson asked. "See anything?"

Jimmy shook his head.

"It just goes on forever."

Dan joined Jimmy and Anderson at the edge. He examined the hole they had made. Only a lattice of wrought iron was left inside a ragged circle of shattered concrete. He measured the hole with the handle of the sledge and turned to Jimmy.

"What are you thinking, Dan?"

"I'm thinking if we cut the rebar, we can fit through the gap. And maybe get down to the bottom."

"We?" Anderson said. "Fuck that. I ain't going down there. I want no part of that *we*, Dan."

Dan scowled and went back to the tool bag.

Jimmy turned away from Anderson and shook his head.

"What?" Anderson said to Jimmy. "You volunteering to go down there, hero?"

Dan pulled an angle grinder from its case and attached it to the portable generator. He lowered his safety glasses and went to work on the first ancient steel bar. The saw whined as it cut, and sent a waterfall of sparks toward Anderson, which forced him to move.

"Jesus Christ!" Anderson whined. "Thanks for the warning."

Jimmy smiled.

NEARBY, Sarah opened the cooler bag and dug through the contents. Ruth had packed thermoses of coffee, turkey sandwiches, some fruit, and even some of her homemade oatmeal chocolate chip cookies. She even prepared a few sandwiches with lettuce wraps for Anderson who insisted on eating keto, even while on a deserted island.

Sarah poured herself a cup of coffee as Terry and Bryan Kaminski approached the table. Terry took a bottle of water and Bryan snagged a cookie.

Both men carried their hard plastic cases.

"This is taking a lot longer than I thought." Terry said as he nodded toward the well. "I didn't realize the well was this...*fortified*."

"They made this to last, that's for sure." Wayne replied, as he grabbed himself a cup of coffee.

"We are going to go set up our stuff." Terry said, gesturing with the cases.

"What's in there?" Sarah asked.

"A drone." Terry told her. "It's going to map the island after Bryan sets up a temporary internet link."

"Why?" Wayne asked.

"Our engineers want a map of the island. That's what the drone is for. The wifi makes life on the island a little more civilized and it allows me to transmit the images from the drone back home to the office."

"You guys aren't gonna stay?" The Sheriff asked. "Looks like they're almost through the cap."

Terry shook his head, smiling at his brother who looked green already just being on the island.

"Honestly, Sheriff. And I think I speak for both of us." Terry said, "We're gonna pass on the dead leper tour."

"All right, boys." He said. "Be careful. How long you boys need?"

"An hour? Maybe two?"

"Okay, let's have you fellas be back here in two hours." The Sheriff said, eying the tumultuous sky above. "Got a feeling all hell is gonna bust loose soon."

THIRTY-SIX

"I need a high point, something protected." Bryan said.

Terry pointed to the rickety barracks as the sky grumbled above them, and said, "Looks perfect."

Bryan squinted up at the structure that trembled with every roll of thunder.

"Are you serious?" He asked. "It looks like termites holding hands."

"Don't be a pussy." Terry said with a chuckle. "Let's get this done before it really starts to rain. I got a bottle of twenty-six-year old scotch back at the hotel calling my name."

Bryan shook his head and stayed where he was as his older brother moved ahead, still staring at the crumbling monstrosity.

"Seriously, Terry, the place looks ready to collapse."

Terry shot a cursory glance at the barracks and then turned back to his brother.

"You heard the Sheriff, they built this shit to last. You'll be fine. Just be careful and be quick. The faster you're set up the faster I can be done."

Terry clapped his brother on the back and headed off toward the rear of the barracks.

"Why don't you set up the link and I'll fly the drone." Bryan said to his brother's back.

"Sorry, bro." Terry replied over his shoulder. "You're the tech support, remember?"

Bryan gave him the middle finger, but Terry had already slipped through a narrow passageway and disappeared.

BEHIND THE BARRACKS the ground sloped sharply down into a field of grey twisted trees and jutting rocks. Terry stood on the top of a boulder and marvelled at the view.

From this spot he could see three quarters of the island as it sloped away toward the water.

The island was beautiful, but he had to admit that the rock forests were a bit weird though. And he could see that it would be an engineering hassle to say the least. Not to mention the possible legal liabilities.

He shook it off. That was something for the army of lawyers he employed to worry about.

He could almost see the new headquarters. Sleek and modern and built to be an extension of the rugged island. Towering glass and slate coloured walls.

But first things first. The engineers had offered to fly the drone and map the terrain, but he didn't want any snap happy idiots taking pictures of the island and sharing it with his competitors. What he didn't want was a bidding war, and to have the price get driven up so high he was muscled out.

He and Bryan were rich, but there was always someone richer and there were a few people who would buy the island just out of spite. Just so he and Bryan couldn't have it.

That wasn't going to happen.

Terry opened the case and lifted the lid revealing a large drone.

He had practiced with it at his estate in upstate New York and he had gotten pretty good. The wind gusted suddenly and blew him to his right causing him to stumble. Terry found his footing and stared at the darkening sky and hoped that this weather moving in wasn't going to ruin his planned flight.

Bryan better hustle.

He gently lifted the drone from its case and set it down on the stone ground. Terry pushed a few buttons and the machine powered up. Using the controller, he activated the engines and the drone lifted slowly off of the ground.

A large screen display was attached to the controller which recorded everything with the camera, but without the wifi connection he would be flying blind.

Thunder rolled overhead and Terry felt the first fat drop of rain.

"Come on, Bryan." He whispered. "Move that ass."

· · ·

FOR ANOTHER MINUTE after his brother left, Bryan stood where he was and looked up at the crumbling Army barracks. Everything about the building was creepy. From the peeling paint to the boarded-up windows, to the rumbling storm getting closer. It was a nightmare scenario.

Perfect. Bryan thought. *Just fucking perfect.*

He thought about looking for somewhere else to set up. Maybe there was a tall rock formation, that was shielded in some way. But he could hear his brother's voice in his head.

'*No Bryan. You saw the island from the helicopter dummy. There's no better spot than the barracks. Stop being a pussy.*'

"You're the fucking pussy." Bryan whispered to himself. "Flying your stupid drone."

Finally, Bryan stepped forward and grabbed the door handle of the main doors. He yanked on the handle and the door opened three inches before it stopped dead.

Of course there would be a messed up door.

Bryan pulled on the door handle again. It was definitely blocked. Like proper stuck. He yanked again, harder this time. If he couldn't get the door open, he would have to crawl through a window ringed with broken glass. He would probably get Tetanus, he thought, or something worse.

He pulled again, and the door opened a little more. Finally, he set the computer case down and grabbed the handle with both hands. He squared his shoulders and really put both ass cheeks into it. He even propped up one boot against the wall for a little extra leverage and gave it an almighty yank.

Suddenly the door exploded outward. The doorknob came off in Bryan's hand and the chubby IT wizard fell backwards into the dirt in a jumble of limbs.

He scrambled to his feet and looked back toward the well to find everyone except his brother staring at him, and trying not to laugh.

Bryan worked out a smile and dusted himself off. Cool as a cucumber. He didn't have to be a mind reader to know what they were thinking...

"Are you okay?" Dan asked.

"I'm good. Thanks." Bryan said, and waved the door-knob still clutched in his hand toward his little group. "Just fine."

Sarah and the men around the well shook their heads and then Dan fired up the angle grinder again and shot a cascade of sparks over the glossy black surface of the well.

Bryan took a quick peek through the door hanging ajar and then slowly, stepped inside.

THIRTY-SEVEN

Jimmy rigged the tripod above the capstone and attached a wire harness to the lattice of rebar built into the concrete.

Dan used the saw on the final connection and when the saw bit through, the heavy piece of rebar and concrete dangled from the harness.

Jimmy swung the piece aside and let it fall to the side of the well.

Dan, Jimmy and Anderson stood at the edge of the well and leaned over the hole they had created. Dan shined his light down into the depths.

Wayne and Sarah joined them, and elbowed their way through the group to get a closer look.

When Dan finally retreated from the hole Anderson asked, "How deep you think it is?"

Instead of answering him, Dan picked up a chunk of the capstone and held it over the hole.

"Ready?"

Wayne checked his watch and nodded.

Dan let the rock go and they all listened for the crash of it hitting something. Anything. Seconds spun by. But there was nothing.

No sound of the rock landing far below. No dull thump. No splash. It was as if the rock dissolved in the darkness.

"That's fucked up." Jimmy said after a time.

"What?" Anderson said. "What's that mean?"

"I didn't hear anything." Sarah said.

"What? I don't get it." Anderson said again, getting nervous. "So, it's deep right?"

Wayne shifted positions and shined his light a little deeper into the well.

"Just calm down, Andy." Wayne said. "We don't know how deep this sumbitch is. Can't see a damned thing. Who knows how far it goes down?"

"Well, it didn't hit rock." Dan said. "We woulda heard it."

"We didn't hear it 'cause it probably hit something...soft." Wayne replied. "Mud or something..."

"Fuck me." Anderson said. "I thought we woulda heard something."

Wayne pulled his light from the hole and joined the rest of the group.

"So now what do we do?" Dan said, as he eyed the sky. "Couple more hours and this storm is gonna be right on top of us."

"Sooner than that." Wayne told him.

The two men stared at each other, as if reading each other's thoughts.

"We gotta be sure." Dan said finally.

"Sure of what?" Anderson said. "It's an endless pit."

"It's not endless, dummy." Jimmy said.

"Fuck you, all right, Sheriff Junior." Anderson snapped back, drawing a glare from the young deputy.

"We have the high angle gear." Dan said to Wayne. "Might as well use it."

"Fuck that." Jimmy said. "No way."

"What?" Sarah said. "What are we gonna do?"

"I ain't going in there." Jimmy said. "I won't. This is bullshit. There's nothing down there. And if there is... well...just let it be, for fuck sakes."

Wayne eyeballed him, as if to say, *'fucking cool it'*, but Jimmy had already backed away, nervously raking his fingers through his hair.

"Jimmy." Wayne tried. "*Just...*"

"No. This place is fucked." Jimmy said, "And this fucking thing." Jimmy kicked the well scattering shards of concrete everywhere. "Is a goddamn nightmare."

"Jimmy." Wayne said quietly, "I told you we have to be sure."

"And I told you I didn't want to come back here." Jimmy said. "I told you that."

"That's the goddamn job." Wayne roared as he grabbed his son by the shoulders. The two men locked eyes.

"You think I want to be here?" Wayne said. "Now get your shit together and calm down."

They didn't speak for a beat and then finally, Jimmy nodded and Wayne let him go. He left his son next to the open coolers of picked over sandwiches and cookies and rejoined the group.

"Someone's gotta go down there and at least look." Wayne said.

"What about lowering a camera?" Sarah asked, but Wayne was already shaking his head.

"Our cameras aren't great and besides we would need a light source to see anything. It's not going to work."

Wayne's gaze swept over Anderson, Sarah and Dan.

"We don't have to do this." He said finally. "I can call a forensic team in from the city or even a team from the university, and they can go down."

"Yeah." Anderson said. "That. Forensic team. Let's do that."

"But it will take some time." Wayne told them.

"How much time?"

"Could be a month, maybe more."

Anderson deflated. "A month?"

"It might be more." Wayne said. "And until then, I would have to seal off the well as a potential crime scene."

"Are you fucking kidding me?" Anderson spat.

Wayne stepped closer to the younger man and stared into his eyes.

"I look like I'm kidding you."

"No." Anderson told him, as he found somewhere else to look.

"I'll go." Dan said.

Sarah's head snapped toward Dan.

"What? No fucking way. No one should be going down there, Dan." Jimmy said. "You don't know what's down there."

"Jimmy." Wayne said. "Why don't you check on the boat, okay? Make sure it hasn't drifted away on us, yeah?"

"You should just call in a forensic team, Dad. Seriously." Jimmy told him.

"Just go check on the boat." Wayne said. "Everything will be fine."

Jimmy stared at the group around the well as he collected himself.

"This place is wrong."

"Okay, Jimmy. Just relax. Everything is gonna be fine."

Jimmy shook his head and shuffled off through the archway and disappeared into the rock forest.

When he was gone Sarah asked Wayne, "Is he all right?"

"He's fine. Been under a lot of stress is all. This place really rattled him. But he'll be all right."

Wayne turned back to Dan.

"You still game to do this, son?"

THIRTY-EIGHT

Inside the barracks the gloom was oppressive. The darkness clung to Bryan, wrapping him in shadows like a wet blanket. He switched on his flashlight and swept the beam over the moldering, rotting interior and groaned. *Of course it stinks in here too.*

Water pooled on the floor rotting through the wood and collecting in brackish ponds feeding mounds of green and black fungus. The walls were scabbed with peeling paint, the plasterboard beneath exposed and cracked.

"This is a bad idea." Bryan whispered to himself. "A very fucking bad idea."

His first step kicked a beer can that spiralled into the darkness. The tinny sound of the can tumbling over garbage was as loud as rifle fire in the darkness.

Bryan swore and waited for the echoes to cease.

The can, he saw, had landed in one of the dirty puddles and was floating lazily. With his breathing in check, he took a shuffling step toward the stairs and heard something else. He paused.

Scratching.

Christ. Rats. And big ones by the sound of it.

"This place just gets better and better."

Bryan waited, then took another step, and the scratching grew louder. He aimed his flashlight at the rotten mound of paper thin mattresses soaked and bloated by the rain and the cold. The mattresses were blocking the stairway and seemed to be the source of the scratching sounds.

He purposefully stomped the last few steps hoping to scare the little buggers into silence, and he did, but now he wondered if that was worse, because there was no way around the heap of mattresses, except over them. He certainly wasn't going to move them by hand.

"Fuck me."

Gently, he grabbed the banister and planted his size ten boot on the soft pile of filthy material and took his first step. His boot sunk into the mound, the sodden mattresses swallowing his leg almost to the knee. The pressure on the nest of rats elicited an insectile shriek. Rats the size of Chihuahuas exploded from their nest in shrieking terror.

Bryan screamed and jumped over the blockade of mattresses stepping on tails and kicking rats aside as he scrambled up the stairs in a panic. The wooden risers moaned under his weight, but the stairs held. His shaking light caught the last of the furry flood as the rats scrambled into the darkness looking for a new hiding place.

"Fuck!" Bryan spat. "Fuck this place!"

He could feel his heart hammering in his ears, and he couldn't catch his breath. He gripped the balustrade and focused on happy things. He thought of his girlfriend Miranda back home. The way she looked in the Valentine's Day lingerie. The way her eyes flashed gold in the firelight. He started to calm down.

Fucking rats.

An errant squeak and the sound of scratching made him look down and he saw a particularly long rat try desperately to climb the riser he was standing on.

"What the hell?"

Furious now, Bryan stepped down onto the same riser and kicked the rat. It spun backward, hit a lower step and landed on the pile of mattresses before righting itself and scampering away. He tried to think of Miranda again, but the moment was gone.

"Fuck this place."

Angry and scared, and angry that he was scared, he focused on the task at hand. He glared up at the stairs and began to climb. He needed to get higher, as high as possible, for the link to work.

As he climbed, dragging himself higher and higher, his hand sliding over the banister he heard more scratching in the walls to his right. They sounded big. Too big.

He did his best to ignore the scratching in the walls and climbed to the top of the stairs. With his back covered in sweat, he wheezed and slightly bent over as he stood on the third floor landing.

To his left was a grand double wide doorway. The doors had long since fallen into disrepair. The right side door was entirely missing, and the left hung by one lone hinge. But through the doorway he saw that there were church pews arranged across the floor in messy rows.

Bryan stepped into the doorway and saw a painting of a penitent Jesus still hung against the far wall. Mold and rot had infected the canvas, like everything else in this building, but he could still see the pain and the agony in the man's face. The rot and the ruin dragged the saviour's eyes down and turned his mouth to a screaming black hole.

"Jesus." Bryan muttered.

CHAPTER
THIRTY-NINE

Rose was nearly frozen as she hustled through the rock forest. Sean was always just ahead of her. He led her, but he didn't stay with her. And he wouldn't talk to her, no matter how much she begged, and she was scared.

The rocks that jutted out of the ground were scary and black and looked like the edges of knives. The thunder grumbled overhead, and she felt the ground shake through her rubber boots.

Fat drops of rain splattered the top of her hood, and she wanted nothing more than to go back to Ruth's house. Back to the cookies and the cool new video game Bryan let her play. She opened her mouth to call out to Sean, but his narrow back disappeared around a corner. Rose hurried to catch up.

Another turn and she found herself on a small stone hill looking down on a massive creepy building. It looked exactly like a haunted house. The kind with broken windows and broken doors. She imagined there would be rats inside as well as giant spiders and other bugs she didn't even want to think about.

Sean stood next to a ground floor window staring at her. When she saw him, he smiled and he waved for her to join him.

Rose shook her head. She knew what he wanted. He wanted her to go inside.

In her head she whispered, *"Please...I don't wanna go in there..."*

Even though she didn't whisper the words out loud she knew that Sean had heard them. He heard everything. She watched his smile fade. His eyes grow dark.

Her skull suddenly exploded with screams. She clapped her hands to her ears to drown out the noise, but the shrieks of pain and madness were inside her head. There was no escape.

The screaming went on and on. She recognized her high-pitched mother's screams mixed in with her father's pleading voice. Desperate, guttural wails that made goosebumps crawl all over her skin and froze the breath in her lungs.

"Okay, okay!" Rose said out loud. "Okay!"

Instantly the screaming stopped. She opened her eyes and saw that Sean's smile was back. Rose dropped her hands from the side of her head.

She climbed down the boulder and joined her brother at the edge of the barracks. Next, Rose followed

Sean through a broken window. She watched her dead brother slip into the darkness and disappear as if he were made of the same stuff.

FORTY

Deputy Jimmy Roberts emerged from the rock forest onto the beach and swept his light over the *Gypsy*. It was where it should be, bobbing in the water, but something was wrong.

It was out too far.

Panicked, Jimmy shined the light on the rock where he had tied up the boat and saw that the rope was still there, but the end was cut. He ran to the rope and saw that...*holy shit.*

The rope wasn't cut. It looked chewed. The frayed end burst from the end of the pristine rope like a weird wiry flower.

"Son of a bitch."

Jimmy dropped the rope and aimed his light at the boat. It was drifting out to sea.

"Son of a bitch!"

If the boat got away, they would have to spend the night on the island and that was not fucking happening.

Jimmy swore again and started stripping off his clothes. He would definitely need something warm to change into once he got the boat back to the shore.

He peeled off his gloves, hat and coat and was working on his jeans when thunder rolled overhead.

"Of course there's a storm." He muttered. He kicked off his boots and dragged his jeans down and piled everything under his coat, protecting it from the inevitable rain.

Wearing only his underwear Jimmy stepped down to the freezing water lapping at the shore. His feet were pinched and poked by shards of granite, as he swore a blue streak the whole time.

"Shoulda been a fucking fireman." He said and without another thought, dove headfirst into the surf.

The freezing water caused his body to spasm, and he exhaled the last of his air in a wet gush, but he swam like the Devil was chasing him. With the storm threatening to drop right on his head and the boat drifting out to sea, his arms and legs churned through the water with machine precision.

His head broke the surface and he spotted the *Gypsy*.

Christ, it had drifted another fifty feet since he last saw it.

Jimmy thrust his head in the water and kicked. He tore at the water and angled his attack. Fifty feet away from the beach and he was already exhausted.

Lightning tore at the sky above, a hooked claw that scratched at the rain filled clouds.

The *Gypsy* twisted in place, caught in a swirling

current, and pointed its stern straight at him. As if daring him to reach her.

Jimmy saw the skinny silver ladder bolted to the right side and powered toward it. Beyond his arms and legs pounding away and clawing at the water he heard the roll and click of the cabin cruiser growing closer. He peeked his head out and there she was. Five feet away.

Jimmy gave it one last kick, grabbed the ladder and hauled himself up and over the side.

"Holy shit!" He cried. "Holy fucking shit!"

His whole body was scrubbed red from the cold and shivering. His hands were curled into claws and he could barely catch his breath.

He used the stairs to reach the lower bunk cabin and splashed into the knee-deep water. The *Gypsy* was sinking.

"No...no...no..."

Pieces of soaked clothing, safety equipment and empty beer cans floated in the dark water. And the water was rising.

Jimmy found a blanket folded neatly on one of the overhead racks and dragged it down. He wrapped the blanket over his shoulders and ran up the stairs to the captain's seat. He sat behind the steering wheel and switched on the radio and found the emergency frequency.

"Mayday...mayday...mayday...this is Deputy James Roberts of the Oak Bay Police Service...is there anyone reading this?"

Static screamed over the radio frequency. Jimmy

switched to a different channel and tried again. Still nothing.

The key still hung from the ignition, and he gave it a twist. The engine coughed and sputtered but didn't turn over.

"Come on."

Jimmy tried the key again and this time the engine fired right up.

Jimmy felt a small smile crawl onto his lips. Thank God for small victories. He reached down into the console on the left side of the driver's seat. A place where he knew his father kept a tiny bottle of Canadian Club. He dug his frozen fingers around the bottom of the captain's chair until his fingers found the glass bottle.

There was barely a swallow left in the bottom, but Jimmy gulped it all. The booze wouldn't help for long, but it still felt good. The amber liquid slid down his frozen throat and exploded in his stomach, setting the meagre contents (half a breakfast burrito) on fire.

"Better than a hot cup of coffee." He whispered to himself.

Finished, he tossed the empty bottle down on the deck and pushed the throttle forward. The twin engines whined and sounded choked. He heard a crash and the engine shuddered and died.

"What the hell?"

Jimmy stood and stomped to the opposite end of the boat, to the stern, where a few lounge chairs were stacked and strapped to the deck. Did they hit something? A rock? He swept his flashlight over the floor of the deck and froze.

At the stern, a thin grey arm slid over the edge of the boat. Long delicate fingers of its hand splayed out and grabbed the edge of a lounge chair.

Jimmy's breath caught in his throat, and he couldn't move. He couldn't breathe. He stared at the shape as another hand slid over the rail. Pale, greasy skin, wrapped in a thin shroud.

And then another.

And another.

Finally, Jimmy found he could move and ran as fast as he could to the rear of the boat. He didn't make it.

Around the entire edge of the back deck ragged, bulging figures were climbing into the boat. Ghastly shapes covered in weeping sores and dripping blisters. They stared at him with ebony eyes, their hollow faces decorated in lesions and scabs.

A small child, no bigger than the little girl Rose, slipped over the edge of the stern onto the deck.

Jimmy gasped but couldn't look away. She stared at him through her shroud. Her features were a wet blur beneath the rotten material. She opened her mouth and a horrific shriek exploded from the tiny girl's throat. A scream that wasn't fear.

It was rage.

It was a war cry.

Jimmy spun and ran for the front of the boat. He couldn't even see the island anymore and he didn't care.

He threw off the blanket he had wrapped around himself, stepped up on the rail and jumped.

The ocean rose to meet him, and he hit the freezing water awkwardly. His bare body slapping a surface that felt like concrete.

He clawed through the water and his fingers closed on a gauzy material. He opened his eyes as a rotten face swam into focus. Flaps of ruined skin hung from its skull as bony fingers reached for him.

Jimmy kicked for the surface but his legs were wrapped, caught in the netting of the shrouds. He kicked and screamed, as bubbles exploded all around him. Through will alone he broke the surface. Gasping, he sucked in a lungful of air as lightning flashed.

He wasn't alone.

He spun in place and saw the crowd of infected that had followed him into the water. They circled him like sharks, closing in. Reaching for him.

Jimmy wasted no time. He eyed a gap in their ranks and kicked and clawed for the safety of the island in the distance.

Skeletal hands slipped over his ankles and pulled him back. Jimmy screamed and kicked harder, but more hands slipped over his body. They trapped his legs and arms, and held them still as sharp fingers pushed into his eyes and filled his mouth.

Jimmy tried to scream but his throat filled with seawater as he slipped beneath the surface. More hands gripped and pulled and tore at his flesh, until Jimmy could feel them inside him. Under his flesh, ripping and tearing.

Lightning strobed overhead one last time and Jimmy saw that the water around him had turned red, as he was dragged deeper, away from the light and into the frozen dark.

FORTY-ONE

Anderson shivered, his arms coiled across his chest as he watched Dan being helped into the climbing harness.

"This is crazy, Dan." Anderson said, and not for the first time.

"You wanna wait a month?" Dan asked him.

"No, but...still."

Wayne did his best to ignore Anderson and told Dan to hold his arms out so he could examine him. After two passes they nodded to each other and deemed everything to be clicked and connected as it should be.

Wayne played out the high tension wire from the tripod and connected the clip to Dan's harness.

Sarah handed Dan a helmet affixed with a camera and a built-in flashlight and he strapped it onto his head.

"Good thing they have an extra large one of those." Sarah told him.

"Jokes? Really?" Dan said.

"I'm nervous." She said.

"You're nervous?"

She slid closer to him and held his face in her hands.

"Just be careful." She whispered. Dan nodded. "And if there's anything…anything at all, let us know and we're out of here. Okay?"

Dan gave her a quick kiss and said, "Okay honey."

"We ready?" Wayne asked.

"Ready." Dan told him.

"Fucking crazy." Anderson muttered as he shuffled away.

"Shut up." Sarah hissed at him. *"Christ."*

Following Wayne's lead, Dan positioned himself up onto what remained of the capstone and then let his feet dangle through the tiny hole.

"The hole looked a lot bigger when I cut it." He said. "Cold in there."

The small group edged closer to the well and Sarah peered into the darkness.

"Now, I'm serious Dan." Wayne told him. "If there's anything hinky at all, I want you to use your radio and call to us, and we'll hoist you right up out of there."

"How much cable do you got?" Anderson asked, and was answered by a glare from Wayne.

"What?" Anderson asked.

"Enough." Wayne told Anderson, and then to Dan, "Just be careful. You're just going down to take a peek. That's all."

Dan nodded. He could already feel his heart ramping up, pounding painfully in his chest. He stared down between his feet and saw the palpable darkness below. It didn't look real. It reminded him of something heavier than just darkness. It reminded him of water. Of outer space. He could feel his lungs tightening. Constricting. His whole body was clenching.

Maybe this was a bad idea...

Dan shook it off and shifted until only the edge of his ass was on the lip of the capstone.

"You sure about this?" Sarah asked him.

"No." He said. "You wanna go?"

She smiled and shook her head, unable to stop the tears from falling.

"I'm sorry." She said, wiping her eyes. "It'll be fine."

"I know." He told her.

Sarah leaned over and kissed her husband. He smelled the coconut shampoo in her hair and felt her cool skin and wanted more.

He watched her as she stared down into the well and then stepped back from the edge.

"You are one brave motherfucker, Dan Avernus." Anderson told him and Dan gave him a nod.

"Listen to your radio, Dan." Wayne said. "And don't unclip from the wire."

"I'll be on the radio too." Sarah told him.

Dan mouthed, *love you.*

"Just get in there, and then get your ass out, okay?" She told him.

"Yes ma'am."

• • •

Wayne started the winch and the cable spooled out. After a moment's hesitation, Dan allowed himself to slip off the edge of the capstone.

For a breathless second Dan knew that the wire would not be able to hold his weight. He had a vision of the wire snapping, or the clip that attached the wire to his harness, breaking apart, and his body falling through the darkness without end.

In the end, he twisted sideways and rolled onto his stomach and let his legs dangle in the open air. With enough wire unspooled, Dan lowered himself over the edge until the wire grew taut and caught him. The edges of the harness bit into his thighs, but the wire held.

He gripped the thin cable with his gloved hands and spun in a lazy circle as the winch whined above him and lowered him into the darkness.

Dan shined his light over the shiny black interior as the winch dropped him inch by inch.

On the screen, the walls of the well were shiny black volcanic glass. Not stone and mortar, but it appeared the well was a single tube of glass and just as smooth.

Dan's breath formed clouds that wreathed his head. His radio crackled and Sarah's voice reverberated off the glossy surface.

"You all right?"

"Perfect." Dan replied.

Dan craned his head to peer up at the top of the well, and saw the tiny aperture where he had come from. It looked like a keyhole and for a second he felt like Alice in Wonderland. He switched his view and aimed his light straight down into the darkness and saw only black.

His stomach did a greasy forward roll.

This was a bad idea, he thought.

FORTY-TWO

Bryan chose his steps carefully.

The floor looked like an unmade bed with the cheap floor tiles buckled and bent, sticking up from the rotten floorboards.

As light as he could manage, Bryan tiptoed across the floor that creaked and moaned with every one of his steps. The entire structure felt ready to collapse.

He turned away from the chapel and entered a narrow hall that led to small, separate rooms. Possibly the Officer's quarters by the looks of them. In each room the ruined remains of soiled mattresses, the remnants of ancient bonfires, and other garbage was strewn about everywhere.

He shuffled slowly down the hallway. Doorways opened to his right and left, and he probed the darkness as he passed. Movement on his left made him flinch and he speared the darkness with his light. His beam pinned a rotting chest of drawers leaning against the wall.

He waited.

Nothing moved.

Just more garbage.

Just more rats, probably.

Bryan shook it off and kept moving forward and thought of watching the demolition crew knock this whole building to the ground and smiled.

After he got to the end of the hall, he realized that all of the rooms were pretty much the same, as far as devastation went. He picked the room with the least amount of garbage and set down his case.

He opened the hard plastic container and pulled out the satellite modem, the attached router and of course the battery pack.

Bryan switched them on and did a systems check on all three devices. When all three devices were humming along, he logged on to the newly formed wifi network and gave it a name.

When that was done, he stood, dusted himself off and said, "Now let's get the fuck out of here."

DOWN ON THE GROUND, Terry stood on a boulder overlooking a portion of the rock forest jutting out of the grey island and the dark blue water beyond. Above him he piloted his drone through a series of figure-eights, deep dives, and steep inclines while he waited for the internet connection.

Another minute passed as a few more fat raindrops splattered against his slicker, and he was about to curse out his brother again for taking his sweet ass time with the set-up when his phone chimed.

"Thank God."

Terry hit a button on the complicated remote that ordered the drone to return to HOME, and then pulled out his phone.

An alert popped up on his screen letting him know that a new wifi network had been detected. Terry clicked on the link and he was asked if he would like to access the network named: TERRY IS A DICK.

"What an asshole." Terry whispered with a smile, and clicked YES.

Soon the drone rose into the darkening sky and began to methodically sweep east and west efficiently mapping the entire island.

While keeping one eye on the display monitor mounted to the remote, Terry moved after the drone. Careful of his footing on the slick rock, he stepped down the slimy stone and headed across the sparse field and down into the rock forest.

Above, the storm was getting worse, darkening the sky and crushing out the daylight.

The images on the screen sent back from the drone showed a line of twisted grey trees. Terry stopped and adjusted the drone, dropping its speed and lowering its angle until he could creep in on the line of weird growths.

The trees were bent and twisted like the spines of elderly skeletons strung up to bleach in the spray of the Pacific. Terry moved the drone back and began to raise its altitude when a gray arm peeled away from the tree.

At first it looked as if a branch had somehow come loose from the spindly tree, but it wasn't a branch. It was an arm. An arm belonging to a person.

Terry's nervous fingers smeared over the buttons that controlled the drone and the little craft bobbed and weaved as Terry found its balance and steadied the craft.

Was it an arm?

Terry studied the screen now, but couldn't see it. Did he imagine it?

He dialed back the speed and slowly pushed the drone closer to the tree where he (thought) he saw the person's arm, until the drone was hovering six feet above the ground.

Terry tapped the image on the screen, increasing the focus. Waiting for something. Tell-tale movement, even audio as the drone was recording in 4K.

But there was nothing. No movement. No sound except for the hush of the surf. Just the weird trees trembling slightly in the wind.

Then he saw it.

His breath caught in his throat as he angled the drone closer. Soon the little boy hiding behind a tree came into view. He was doing his best to hide behind a tree, but Terry spotted him.

"Gotcha."

Terry aimed the drone closer to the boy. He looked to

be about ten, maybe older with dark hair and blue eyes. As the drone drew closer the boy stepped away from the tree and...*was he fucking smiling?*

Terry recognized the *Monster Hunter* t-shirt the kid wore and grinned. Even out here in the sticks, even on a deserted island, the Kaminski Brothers had fans.

On the screen the kid was walking toward the drone, his smile growing wider. He was so close that Terry saw the kid's eyes shift to the left. A second later the drone slammed forward into the rocks. The ground rushed up toward the screen way too fast and then...only blue screen.

"Fuck!"

Terry frantically pressed the buttons on the drone remote but there was nothing. The drone was worth more than some cars he saw drifting around this shit town. If his property was damaged, he was gonna make someone pay. And pay a lot.

He checked the screen on the remote and stabbed more buttons. The screen simply read:

CONNECTION LOST

"Motherfucker!" Terry screamed. "Stupid hicks."

He shuffled around glaring at his phone to pinpoint just where the drone had crashed and finally decided on a path that led him due east toward the edge of the island. Terry checked the sky above growing darker by the second and then pocketed the phone.

"If my shit is ruined, you're so dead, assholes!" He screamed. "*Fucking kids.*"

FORTY-THREE

Dan shined the light down between his legs and still couldn't see the bottom. The tunnel just continued to drop below him, and he wondered what he would do if the hoist ran out of line? What if the tunnel extended to the center of the earth? The idea made him smile. If this well was endless, that would mean there were no bodies down here and that they were in the clear.

He twisted to his left on the wire, the harness creaked and he shivered as the temperature dropped a few more degrees with the depth. It was getting colder down here. He could feel it in his chest and in his lungs. He coughed and it sounded like cannon fire in the close confines.

Even the smallest sounds in the tunnel were amplified by the glossy walls and the smothering dark. The creak of the harness, the barely audible whine of the winch high above, even his breathing blasted off the walls and swirled around him as he dropped in slow motion.

Moments later, his light found a few vertical slashes in the wall to his right and he leaned closer as he was lowered. The three faint lines carved a trio of ragged vertical slashes. As Dan dropped, he followed them with his beam.

Something was stuck in the wall at the end of the far left line. Dan leaned in as close as he could and shined his light on the splinter of a fingernail sticking out of the wall.

Dan swore and reeled back, his body bouncing in the harness. His light swept over the tunnel and he saw more similar scratches.

"Dan? Dan? You okay?" Sarah's voice came over the radio filled with static. "Are you okay?"

For the first time Dan felt the walls closing in on him and the tiny space all around him felt like it was collapsing in on him. Squeezing him. He struggled to breathe. Everything felt wrong and still he dropped into the endless dark.

Sarah's voice cut through the static on the radio, "Dan? Answer me."

"I'm okay." He said finally. "I'm fine."

"What was that?"

He thought about telling her, but decided against it.

"It's fine." He said. "It was nothing."

There was silence on the line and then Sarah was back, "Can you see anything yet?"

Dan nodded to himself. He'd seen too much already.

With his breathing under control, he peered through his dangling feet. For the first time his light reflected off something far below.

"There's something." He said into his radio. "I think I found the bottom."

The closer he got, he saw it more clearly. The tunnel ended and beyond the edge of the glossy tube he was slowly lowered into a massive subterranean cavern.

He was nearing the bottom. The floor was slowly coming into view, and it was covered in bones.

"Jesus Christ." Dan whispered.

"We're...hope...cable..." Sarah's voice was garbled with static and he could barely hear her. But it didn't matter, because Dan couldn't speak. He continued to drop until his feet landed softly on what remained of a pile of dead bodies wrapped in rags.

Shrouds. He thought.

Lepers.

He fumbled with the remote control for the winch but managed to stab the right button and his progression stopped. Yellowed skulls the colour of parchment crumbled beneath his boots as his weight shifted on the pile. Bones wrapped in rotting rags spilled down the sides of the cairn and clattered to the stone floor.

Once he settled, Dan shined his light over the cavernous room he had been lowered into. The stone walls were identical to the tunnel, formed of black volcanic rock. Smooth and seamless. He felt as though he were in the belly of a gigantic beast.

Dan unclipped himself from the cable and picked his

way down to the floor. A handful of bones scattered and rolled in a mini-avalanche as he stumbled onto solid ground.

He swept his light over the pile that he had climbed down. He guessed it would be at least twenty feet wide and ten feet tall.

My God.

It was true. He thought. *The crazy sonofabitch actually did it.*

He nudged the dome of a skull and saw a round hole in the forehead. The pale bone still scorched from the muzzle flash.

These people didn't die. They were executed, and their bodies had been tossed down the well to land in a heap. Disgraced and discarded.

Desecrated.

Dan reached for his radio and keyed the talk button. "You're not gonna believe this."

The reply was all static. Dan peered up at the roof and allowed his light to reach as far as it would go and still, he could barely see the stalactites reaching down for him like jagged teeth.

Dan moved in a daze away from the main pile beneath the well entrance and saw the remains of people that must not have died outright. He shuffled closer and saw a small skeleton, withered and mummified, curled into the lap of a larger form.

Some of these people weren't dead when they were thrown in.

He moved deeper into the auditorium and quickly

found more skeletons leaning against the smooth wall. Some facedown and scattered as if an animal had torn them apart.

His breath was coming faster now, and the clouds it formed wreathed his head. The darkness was oppressive, and he could feel eyes on him like a physical weight. This place was wrong. So very wrong.

Dan shifted backward toward the hill of bones, toward the winch line, when his light swept over the wall to his left.

The wavy, ebony wall was scarred with a multitude of wounds. Scratches and grooves were carved into the shiny surface from the edge of the floor. A single word carved over and over again. A chant. A threat. A warning.

AVERNUS

A subtle noise, the clatter of rocks, drew Dan's headlamp to the right. The strong white beam reflected off the pools of water that had begun to swell around the mound of remains. But that couldn't be right. There was no water on the ground. Not when he had first arrived. He was sure of it.

Dan kept his light pinned to the largest puddle, about ten feet in front of him, as the water continued to rise as the puddle spread out farther and farther.

"What the hell?"

The water rose, faster and faster. It swept thick and black over the floor of the cavern as it joined the other, smaller puddles, to form a brackish, ebony tide.

Dan picked his way around the rising water and began to climb the burial mound. He scrambled up the small hill, grabbing onto femurs and palming yellowed skulls as he made his way higher and higher toward the loose coil of cable.

He shot a glance back toward the cavern and saw that the entire floor was now covered in dark water.

Oh my god...

Dan froze. Every fibre of his being told him to keep climbing. To get out. But he couldn't move. He couldn't look away.

Something was rising out of the water.

Slowly, skeletal forms rose.

Their emaciated forms were wrapped in moldy shrouds. Faces and features blurred by the wet gauze stained with ancient blood stared up at him. The dark pits of their eyes and the hollows of their yawning mouths were laser focused in his direction.

Dan bit back a scream. His hands shook from the fear and the cold, but he managed to scramble up the burial mound and reach the steel clip. He clipped the cable to his harness and stabbed the UP arrow on the winch remote and watched in agony as the cable slowly retracted and grew taut.

His headlamp flicked from left to right as he witnessed the dark water rise incredibly, impossibly fast. In less than a minute the water had climbed a foot up the burial mound.

More and more shrouded figures emerged from the

liquid, assembling as if called to battle. Grey limbed and wrapped in dirty rags.

"Come on. *Come on!*" Dan hissed as he cursed the slowness of the winch.

He eyed the rising water as it quickly devoured the distance between them. Slowly, the harness pulled tight and he was lifted off his feet. He spun in a tight circle, and his light swept over the cavern.

The black tide continued to rise, bringing with it the wraiths that were coming to exact their revenge.

FORTY-FOUR

Terry picked his way across the rocky field littered with boulders. Some were the size of SUVs, and some were bigger still and they all were slick with some sort of black, greasy algae that seemed to soak into his hands no matter how hard he wiped them off.

He took a whiff of his fingers and winced. Whatever the rotten slime was, it smelled rancid.

Terry hopped carefully down from a boulder the size of a Prius and swept his flashlight back and forth across the forest of densely packed trees. When his beam hit the thin, twisted branches, it fractured, and sparked shadows to life as he searched for the fallen drone.

He didn't see it and checked his phone screen. He still had a wifi signal and according to the app the drone should be right where he stood.

But it wasn't.

"You gotta be fucking kidding me...all that money and the fucking thing..."

Terry stepped closer to the edge of the tree line and probed a little deeper with his light until he finally saw it. A piece of metal and plastic glittered in the harsh white light.

"Gotcha." Terry hissed.

About twenty feet into the skeletal forest, he saw what had to be the wreckage of the drone. But how the hell did it get in there? Terry scanned left and right, and the forest wall appeared to be seamless. No gaps. No breaks in the dense weave of the branches.

"This is why I don't have kids." He muttered.

Terry stuffed his flashlight under his arm and held back a pair of spindly, white branches wide enough apart to allow him to step into the gap. He hopped through the opening and pushed through the next five feet of ropy vines barbed with thorns, as he cursed and swore and yelped in pain as the nasty little nettles dug into his skin, tore flesh and drew blood.

Finally, with a vicious thrash of his arms he broke through and found himself in a hollow clearing, approximately twenty feet in diameter.

The walls were identical to the nightmare he just bashed through. A nearly seamless wall of thorny branches, and in the center of the clearing was the ruined drone.

Terry stepped closer to the wreckage and swept his light over his confines. It was much darker in here than on the field. And colder too. The dense roof of the hollow, ten feet above his head, was constructed by a canopy of armored vines that seemed determined to block both the sun's light and warmth. Terry's warm breath formed rags of clouds in the shadows.

He squatted next to the remains and saw that the drone hadn't just been knocked out of the sky. The drone had been obliterated. Pulverized, and then moved into this place.

As bait. His mind screamed at him.

Holy shit.

Terry swept his light over the walls of the hollow and found nothing but shadows. Icy wind whistled through the weave of the trees and the branches, as delicate as wrist bones, clattered together in symphony.

He suddenly felt very alone and exposed. Even with the spotty wifi they had installed, who was he going to call to report this? The Sheriff? He didn't even know where he was exactly. They were alone out here. Help-lessly alone.

Except for the kids who did this. Terry thought, as he nudged the broken bits of the drone with his boot. They were here too. And probably watching him. Laughing at him.

He shined his light over the twisted trees that had looked so cool to him back when he was with the group, back when he could hear their chatter and this trip was all a fun exercise.

The trees looked different now. Stranger. More menacing.

And then they moved.

Along the far side of the hollow, a branch peeled away from its trunk and Terry realized that what he was looking at, was not a tree, but a person. An impossibly thin person wrapped in a filthy, gray shroud.

Its skeletal arm uncoiled from the thin wood of the tree and joined their body that was hidden, just out of view.

Terry's light shook as he panned it across the far wall of the clearing as more people emerged from the shadows. Threading their way through the branches, drawing near. Shuffling closer.

He opened his mouth to say something. Anything, but his mouth felt like it had been filled with sand. He stepped backward and his boots splashed through an inch of murky water.

"What the hell?"

The water hadn't been there before. But it was definitely here now. And it was rising.

Terry aimed his light at the walls of the hollow, and saw that the figures silently climbing through the twisted forest had doubled.

"Who are you?" He said, "You can't be here."

But there was no authority in his words. He didn't care who they were. Not really. He just wanted to be out of there. He wanted to be off this island. He wanted to be home.

Now.

Terry took one last look at the shrouded group inching their way through the twisted trees and ran.

He found the trampled opening he had barrelled

through earlier and dove in headlong. With his arms up to shield his face he kept his head down and stomped as quick as he could through the thorny wall until he emerged into the withering sunlight.

His boot caught on a root and he fell forward, his hands plunging deep into the thick black, putrid water. He gasped and felt his lunch rise up his throat, but he scrambled to his feet. With his clothes soaked, the wind whipping off the ocean knifed into his bones and cut into his skin.

He shot a glance back toward the tree line and saw the shrouded crowd had emerged right behind him.

Terry made a low mewling sound in his throat as he ran. A sound he hadn't made since he was eight and was chased home by Gilly French, the neighbourhood bully that used to give him Indian burns and steal the treats out of his lunch.

Whimpering like a frightened child, Terry ran faster than he had in years. Arms pumping, legs churning, through the boulder field as his feet splashed through the rising tide of dark water.

Scared and confused, he stopped at a towering boulder that had blocked his way. He scanned the way to his right and sloshed in that direction, until his right boot stepped into an unseen hole below the water line. He cried out as his ankle buckled beneath his weight with the delicate crack of snapping kindling.

Terry dropped his flashlight as he fell backward into the filthy fluid. Soaked and writhing in pain, his hands immediately probed the area around his stuck right foot, desperate to dislodge it. While, still, the water rose.

"It's not possible." Terry whispered. "It's not possible."

His fingers dug through the muddy soil around his trapped boot, as he wrenched and pulled without success. It was as if he had stepped into a bear trap. Something was holding him.

Fingers slipped over his own and grabbed his wrists. Terry screamed and recoiled. His back arched as he tried to pull his hands away.

"No! NO! NO!" Terry shrieked.

Terry kicked and writhed and thrashed but more and more slender, pale hands snaked out of the bruise coloured water. Sharpened nails pierced his clothes and tore through flesh to anchor into bone.

Terry screamed until he was hoarse.

A forest of white limbs formed around him. They slithered around his frame. They coiled around his head and squeezed with the force of a pneumatic press.

Terry's mind broke along with every bone in his body with a sickening crunch as lightning tore at the sky and formally announced that the storm had begun.

CHAPTER

FORTY-FIVE

Ruth paced relentlessly back and forth across the kitchen floor, threatening to wear a groove in the linoleum as she stared at her old-fashioned wall phone, her thumbnail between her teeth.

A decision needed to be made.

She had checked the house from top to bottom. In every closet and drawer and crawl space a child could hide in.

She didn't live here all these years to have some child hide in a spot she hadn't already discovered. Rose wasn't inside the house. Of that, she was sure.

Ruth then checked the shed, and the back yard, and the beach down by the dock. No, no and no. There was no point in denying it any longer. Ruth knew in her heart where the child was. She was on that goddamn island. Why she was there she didn't know. But ever since Marcus hadn't come home, she got a bad feeling every time she caught sight of the place.

It was an unfamiliar feeling. A coldness she hadn't felt before.

Little Rose was on the island. She was sure of it. As sure as she was of anything.

Finally, she made the decision, yanked the old black handset from the wall, and dialed a number she knew by heart.

Margaret Bleeker, the police dispatcher, answered on the second ring in her usual cheery voice, "Oak Bay Sheriff's office, how can I help you?"

"Margaret, it's Ruth Coolidge."

"Oh hi, Ruth. How's it going over there? The boys back yet?"

"No, they aren't. And I think...well...I think Dan's little girl...she was here. I was supposed to watch her, but I think, I'm not sure..." Ruth stammered. She would screw this up too. She could tell she was losing Margaret. She could almost see Margaret's chubby face scrunched up with concentration, as she tried to follow Ruth's rambling monologue.

"See, Rose was supposed to stay back with me, but when I checked her room, to wake her up, she wasn't there." Ruth said, finally.

"Oh Ruth, did you check the beach?" Margaret asked, "Little kids love the beach."

"I checked the beach, Margaret." Ruth said as she rolled her eyes. "Of course I did. I checked everywhere and she's not here. She's not in the house or outside. I think she's over on the island."

"Well, how would she get there?"

"I don't know." Ruth said, "Maybe she stowed away in the cabin cruiser I..."

"And little Danny is there? On the island?"

"Yeah." Ruth told her. "Danny, his wife Sarah..."

Goosebumps flashed over Ruth's skin and her breath frosted in the air.

When Margaret spoke again her voice was lower. It sounded far away, as if Margaret was holding the phone away from her mouth, speaking into the receiver from across the room. Or from across the ocean.

"*And Rose.*"

Ruth gripped the phone in her hand and heard the plastic creak. Condensation gathered on the mouthpiece and Ruth's panicked breaths bloomed into ragged clouds around her head.

"Margaret?"

Ruth pressed her ear to the phone, listening to the dead air hiss.

"*Margaret...*"

"They're all there now, Ruth." A voice said that was not Margaret's. Ruth's recognized the voice, she would know it anywhere. She had lived with it for decades.

It was Marcus' voice.

"All of them Ruth." He hissed. "Avernus. All of them. All that remain. Avernus."

Marcus dragged out the last word as if he were grinding it between gnashed teeth. As if he were punishing the very name of his nemesis.

"*Aaaaavvvverrrrrrnnnnnnnuussssssssss.*"

"*Please.*" Ruth begged. "Please. *Marcus.*"

A tortured chorus of screams exploded out of the earpiece. Screaming, shrieking voices begging for people to stop, to please have mercy, to let them go.

A symphony of screams. Mindless and terrified. Haunted and in pain all wailing at once.

Ruth dropped the phone as if it were a slithering cobra and stumbled away and stared at the black plastic handset swinging on the end of its coiled cord as it swept back and forth, bumping against the wall.

The tortured voices continued to chant.

To beg.

To plead in vain.

"Please! Please! Please!"

FORTY-SIX

Rose was tired and cold and scared inside the barracks. The rotting wood and the moldy bits of clothes and old mattresses all smelled like pee to her, and she was pretty sure she could hear the sharp little claws of rats as they scurried around behind the walls.

She didn't want to touch anything, but the higher she climbed on the stairs the more unstable the risers became. She was halfway up to the second floor when the stair beneath her boots collapsed, and her little left foot punched through the rotten wood.

She bit back the scream that threatened to explode from her throat and grabbed the wobbly banister with both hands as hot tears pricked at the corners of her eyes.

Above her on the landing, her dead brother Sean stared down at her. A small smile on his lips. A flare of white hot anger bloomed inside her chest and Rose hated him in that moment.

Without saying a word, she knew what he wanted, and there was no negotiation. So, she gently pulled on her stuck boot until she freed her foot and finished the climb to the second floor.

Atop the stairs, she found herself on a large landing that led to a double-wide arched doorway. She crept over the dusty floorboards into an ancient dining hall.

In the centre of the landing a small, perfectly round puddle of dark liquid had formed. Rose stared at it curiously, because it didn't look like water. It looked more like oil and the puddle was growing larger.

She watched in fascination as the puddle spread silently across the ruined floorboards and forced her backward into the dining hall.

The puddle stunk like the time they found a dead raccoon under their shed last July. But beyond that, there was something wrong with the liquid. Just looking at it made Rose's stomach turn over.

Rose shuffled backward until she was through the doorway and away from the dark water. She spun around, and studied the room, and realized that the only way out, was now blocked by that pool of black fluid.

Broken tables and chairs were scattered throughout the wide open space as wagon wheel chandeliers wrapped in thick spiderwebs dangled precariously above.

"Sean?" She whispered. "Sean? I wanna go home. Please, I don't wanna be here anymore."

But her brother was gone. There was only garbage and broken furniture in this large empty space. Lightning flickered across the dusty windows and energized an army of shadows. Thunder soon followed and the chandeliers trembled and dropped bits of dirt and plaster dust to the floor.

"Sean?" She asked weakly. "Are you here? Where's Mom?"

Rose moved to the windows, careful not to step under the chandeliers, and peered down into the courtyard. There, far below she saw a small group standing around what looked like a well. Her heart leapt when she spotted her mother's copper-colored ponytail.

"Mom! MAMA!" She squealed. "Mama!"

Rose hurried to the window and slammed her palm on the glass.

"Mama! Up here!"

But there was no way she could hear her. Not through the window. And just as she thought, the small group far below didn't so much as twitch in her direction. She bit her bottom lip and stared at the huge windows.

She had an idea.

Rose scrambled back toward the far wall where a large wooden table sat awkwardly on the floor, with only three of its legs still attached. She smiled as she lifted the broken table leg and carried it back to the window. It was as heavy as her brother's old baseball bat and about the same shape. Excitement and fear spiked her bloodstream as she approached the glass deciding how best to do this.

She told herself it was for a good cause, and no one would care about a smelly old building anyways.

With her conscience intact, Rose gripped the table leg like a Louisville Slugger and after three short practice swings, she let the chunk of wood fly and immediately covered her face.

The heavy wooden missile rocketed through the floor to ceiling window and sent a shower of glass down onto the courtyard.

FAR BELOW ANDERSON, Wayne and Sarah jumped as the table leg bounced on the stony ground and came to rest amid the broken glass.

Anderson pointed to a second floor window where Rose's small form edged toward the gap.

"Holy shit." He said to Sarah. "Isn't that your kid?"

Before Sarah could respond, Rose's high keening voice knifed through the growing darkness, "*MAMA!*"

Sarah's eyes snapped to the open window.

"Oh my god!"

"Is that Rose?" Wayne asked. "How did she get here?"

But Sarah didn't bother trying to tackle questions she had no answers to. It didn't matter how her daughter got here. She was here, and now it seemed, she was in trouble.

"Hey, what the hell is she doing here, Sarah?" Anderson said. Again, Sarah ignored him as her eyes flicked from the well to the looming barracks.

"I don't know! I have no idea!" She snapped as she dug through the mess of tools for a flashlight.

"Just go." Wayne told her. "We can take care of Dan. Go get your kid. But be careful in there. Whole place is ready to cave in on itself."

Sarah nodded and took off running.

"Stay right there, honey." Sarah called to her daughter. "I'm coming."

CHAPTER

FORTY-SEVEN

Bryan's head whipped around to the sound of breaking glass. He crept to his own window on the third floor. Then he heard the scream. High and piercing it sounded like it came from right below him. It sounded like a little girl.

Why would a little girl be on the island?

He stood very still and waited for another scream, and when he heard it, another voice followed. This one farther away, but he could still pick out what the woman said.

"Rose..."

Bryan wondered how the little girl he met yesterday had managed to come to the island on her own, but quickly gave up. To him kids were a complete mystery.

Having finished what he set out to do up here in this nightmare of a building, he decided to go check out what all the screaming was about.

He was halfway to the door when a tide of black, filthy water swept into the room. Bryan winced, and held up his hand and covered his mouth and nose.

"Oh, what the shit is this?"

Maybe a pipe had burst? But there were no pipes. This building hadn't had plumbing in seventy years. Still, the sludge continued to advance. It spread out from the doorway in a slow, greasy wave and forced Bryan to step backward.

"What the hell?"

The dirty water quickly spread across the floorboards, the murky puddle growing outward at an alarming rate. The black fluid flowed through the doorway, into the room, and forced him back toward the windows overlooking a narrow balcony.

Bryan shined his flashlight on the water as a ripple trilled across the surface. His breath caught in his throat.

Pale fingers curled out of the viscous fluid and reached for the floorboards.

"Oh...you gotta be fucking kidding me...Jesus Christ..."

The fingers were followed by slender hands and arms. Limbs corrupted by weeping lesions and dripping sores and draped in filthy shrouds.

"Nononononononno..." Bryan whispered. "This isn't happening. This isn't fucking happening."

But it was happening, and the black sludge had crept to within ten feet of where Bryan stood. Soon, Bryan's ass bumped against the windowsill behind him. He had nowhere to go. He tore his eyes away from the horror that was crawling out of the black water and shifted his attention to the window. He tried to raise it, but the wood was warped or painted shut, or both. It was stuck. It wouldn't budge.

Bryan shot a glance over his shoulder and saw the first shrouded horror slowly rise to its feet. Pus and blood and God knows what else was smeared across the fabric of the filthy rags it wore. It turned its featureless head toward him and Bryan could see the black pits of its eyes behind the shroud. The points of sharpened teeth winked in the weak light behind its dirty veil.

"Fuck! No!"

Bryan returned and tried the window again, as tears streamed down his face. He pushed as hard as he could on the window frame. The ancient wood creaked, but didn't give.

"Come on! Come on!"

He tried again and again as the smell of the rancid liquid filled the room like a fog.

"Fuck it!" Bryan hissed and grabbed his laptop from the floor. With a single fluid motion, he smashed out the window glass.

He stuck his head out of the window and found a small balcony on the floor below.

"Shit...*shit*..."

No choice.

Bryan swung his legs out over the window ledge. His hands crunched over bits of broken glass and he could feel the tiny shards bite through his skin, but he held firm. He shifted his weight until he was hanging from the window.

He dangled as long as he could, as blood seeped out between his fingers until he finally let go.

Bryan landed hard on the second floor balcony. His weight, combined with the ten foot drop, forced the bolts that held the railing to the wall, to pop free, and the entire balcony tilted out toward the stony ground below. The platform creaked and groaned as it tore free from the building.

Wheezing and bleeding, Bryan scrambled on all fours to the broken balcony doors and dove through the ragged gap.

As quick as he could, he scurried across the rotten floorboards, just as the ruined balcony behind him fell away, and landed below with a thunderous crash.

Bryan rolled over onto his back and stared up at the cracked plaster ceiling as he tried to control his breathing. It had been years since he moved that quickly and his body was not used to it. His physical fitness activity consisted of moving from the bed to the desk, to the couch.

Everything hurt and he felt like he could sleep for a week. His pulse throbbed in his neck, and he raised his hand to feel the artery in his throat that was no doubt bulging and receding against his skin in a rapid drumbeat.

But his hand wouldn't cooperate.

He felt freezing cold water soak through the seat of his jeans and the shoulders of his jacket. Bryan suddenly couldn't breathe. He tried to jerk his back off the floorboards, but he was stuck. He felt welded in place.

Frigid water climbed higher over his body and the disgusting stink of sewage and rot filled his nostrils, and he gagged.

"Help! Help me!" Bryan screamed. "Rose! Anyone please!"

Delicate fingers climbed over his frozen form like hundreds of centipedes. Across his knees, over his thighs, his groin, and higher.

Sharp fingernails scratched across his throat and carved shallow grooves in the thick flesh of his cheeks.

"No please no please no please no..."

The water rose higher. The putrid liquid moved with its own physics, against gravity to cover his body completely as the hundreds of fingers and hands increased their grip.

Bryan felt a finger probe close to his mouth and he squeezed his lips shut and clenched his teeth as he prayed to any god that was listening.

Intense pressure stole the breath from his lungs as the hands of the dead pulled down on Bryan's body, determined to pull him through the floor.

Bryan felt the bones of his left forearm snap with a sickening crack, and he opened his mouth to scream. Immediately, sharp fingernails swarmed into his mouth and burrowed down his throat as the pressure increased.

Bryan gagged and bucked and writhed as more bones broke. His chest collapsed with the snap of kindling and a wheeze of wasted breath. And then, with a final yank, Bryan's shattered body disappeared completely. Pulled beneath the glossy black surface of the dark water. Leaving barely a ripple in his wake.

FORTY-EIGHT

Inside the well, Dan rose excruciatingly slowly. He kept his light pinned on the space between his feet and watched the mountain of bones slowly drift out of view as the shadows thickened between them.

Far below he heard the clatter of the skulls and femurs shifting as they knocked together. Something was coming.

Dan angled his flashlight at the sound, and saw that the mound of bones hadn't been covered by shadow, but by water. He saw ripples ruffling its surface as he rose. The water was rising fast.

Too fast.

Dan stared up at the tiny keyhole aperture that was the entrance to the well and his heart dropped. At the rate the cavern below was filling, he wouldn't make it.

He gripped the radio and pushed the talk button.

"Sarah?"

Static exploded from his walkie and then after a brief pause, it was Wayne's voice he heard.

"Dan? You all right?"

Dan shined his light down at the bottom of the well, and the far reach of his beam caught the water as it lapped against the ceiling of the cavern, and the beginning of the well.

"Dan? You all right?" Wayne asked. "Talk to me, son."

"Hey." Dan said. "Can you hear me?"

"What did you see?"

Dan ignored Wayne's question and said,"Listen to me the water is rising."

"What?" Wayne asked. "What water?"

"The water in here. It's rising." Dan said. "You gotta be ready to seal the well as soon as I clear the capstone."

Dan heard nothing, and then Anderson was on the radio.

"What are you talking about, Dan? What did you see?"

Dan stared down, shining his light on the rising, filthy sewage that was closing the gap.

"I don't have time for this, Anderson!" He shouted. "Just get ready to close the fucking thing! There are people down here! Just be fucking ready!"

Dan stabbed the UP button on the winch remote as his heart beat against his ribs like a frightened bird. His breath clouded the air around his head in the frigid tube as he watched in horror as the water rose between his feet.

His flashlight hand shook uncontrollably, but it

didn't matter. He could still clearly see the veiled face of the skeletal figure that stared up at him from the surface of the black water.

Dan stared up at the opening in the capstone as the sound of the winch motor grew louder and louder.

Come on...come on...

Less than twenty feet below his feet, Dan could hear the thick, syrupy water slosh against the smooth sides of the well.

Below him, the shrouded figure was joined by four more, until the well below him was filled to capacity. As one, they raised their withered arms as they reached for him. A desiccated forest of ruined limbs, dripping with brackish water, and blood, and pus. Gnarled fingers, hooked into claws, reached for the soles of his dangling boots.

Dan gasped and lifted his knees to his chest, as the rising tide outpaced the winch motor. He could hear their long nails as their claws clicked together, desperate to sink into his skin and tear flesh and break bones.

Spears of light angled down from the hole in the capstone.

"Dan?" Wayne said.

"Holy shit!" Anderson squealed. "What the fuck is that?!"

Dan stared up at the silhouettes of the two men and imagined the confusion and terror on their faces. His thighs burned with the effort of keeping his feet out of the monsters' grasp, but he had no choice.

"Get ready to seal this off!" Dan screamed. "Get ready to pull me out!"

"Dan what the fuck is that?" Anderson said, as his pale face came into view. "What the fuck is that?"

Dan reached up and grabbed the edge of the capstone. As the winch continued to pull him up.

Wayne was there and grabbed Dan's wrists.

"Come on, son." He said. "Move your ass."

Wayne pulled on Dan's wrists as hands closed over Dan's boots.

The motor of the winch whined and smoked, as the weight pulling the cable in the opposite direction was too great.

Dan slipped from Wayne's grasp and shot backwards into the well.

Hands and fingers clawed at Dan's legs, and he could feel hooked nails slice into his skin. He screamed and thrashed as the winch motor inched him up toward the light.

"Hold on, Dan!" Wayne screamed and climbed on top of the capstone and reached down into the well.

"Hold on, goddammit!"

ANDERSON BACKED away from the well, his eyes glazed. His mind reeling from what he had seen. He shuffled a few steps to his left and then to his right, as if unsure exactly where he was or how he got there.

And then he saw the well, and he remembered.

And then he ran for the beach.

DAN REACHED for Wayne and grabbed his wrist, as what felt like a knife sliced across his back. Dan roared in pain as Wayne yanked him through the tiny opening.

Dan scrambled over the capstone and dove for the ground, clawing at his harness as Wayne took one last look at the rising black tide.

Dozens of hollow-eyed faces stared up at him, rising with the black water. Veiled mouths open in a silent scream, talons clicking at the end of rotting fingers, reaching for him.

With a clang, Dan slammed the square piece of metal over the hole in the capstone. Wayne's hands shook as they held the concrete screws in place, but soon Dan joined him with the drill and powered the first one home. Quickly, he fired in the second screw diagonally from the first, as the wave of black sludge flooded up from the well. The putrid fluid splashed over the two men, and they recoiled at the stink.

Dan recovered first and grabbed the third screw. He set it through the pre-drilled hole as a pale hand punched into the metal from below, and knocked the drill from Dan's hands.

The corner of the metal sheet bent upwards as a torrent of thick sludge exploded through the gap.

Dan wiped away the filth from his face and picked up the drill.

"Leave it, Dan!" Wayne screamed, as he pulled Dan away from the well. "Leave it! Christ, we gotta get your family and go."

Pale hands reached through the gap between the metal plate and the capstone. Fingers clawed at the open air, as more and more of the black fluid gushed from the well and pooled on the ground around it.

Dan dropped the drill and spun toward Wayne. He searched the Sheriff's terrified face whose eyes were still pinned to the rushing water.

"What do you mean, family?" Dan asked him, as he scanned the area around the well. They were alone, as freezing rain fell like shards of glass.

"That's...that's not..." Wayne mumbled to himself as he shook his head in disbelief. "No. It's not..."

"*Wayne.*" Dan said, and grabbed the older man by the shoulders. He shook him and Dan saw a flicker of anger bring the Sheriff back from the brink. Wayne shook Dan off and glared at him.

"We gotta go." Wayne said, as his eyes drifted back toward the well. "Now."

But Dan shook his head.

"Wayne, look at me." He said. "Where's Sarah, Wayne?"

FORTY-NINE

nderson ran. He ran like the devil himself was chasing him, and maybe he was.

His flashlight whipped left and right as he dashed through the rock maze in what he hoped was the direction of the pier and the shitty cabin cruiser they came in on.

Anderson turned left and found himself in a dead end, and a screamed curse formed a ragged cloud in the dark. He ran back the way he had come, and this time turned the right way, and followed the sound of the waves as they broke on the beach.

All the while his mind replayed what he had seen in the well. *What he had thought he had seen.* His mind corrected him. What he had actually seen, was probably explainable. Definitely not supernatural. He definitely did not see a crowd of undead lepers reaching out for him through the dark water.

He would get to the boat and demand the stupid,

sarcastic deputy take him back to the mainland. Christ, he would pay him. It didn't matter. He couldn't stay one more second on this island.

His foot tripped on a rock hidden in shadow and he fell forward in a heap. His flashlight spun from his grasp as his chest hit the hard packed ground and he yelped like a kicked dog.

Thunder grumbled above him as Anderson scrambled to his feet. He found his flashlight at his feet, rolling in a lazy spiral against the ground.

He snatched the light from the ground and did a quick sweep, shining the light all around him.

He heard a noise surrounding him that was growing louder. A scratching noise, like fingernails on stone.

Something was coming for him.

Hunting him.

The sound from Anderson's throat was more of a moan than a scream, and it hurt to breathe, but it didn't matter. He took off running through the next turn and the next until the scratching sound was smothered by the roar of smashing breakers.

He stumbled onto the rocky beach, and shot a terrified glance over his shoulder as he pushed his body toward the edge of the water.

Anderson was running so fast that he was knee deep in the surf before he realized the boat was gone.

No.

A high keening sound grew in his throat. A sound he hadn't made since he was a child, terrified in his grandmother's basement when the lone bulb died, and he couldn't find the stairs. Screaming and crying with piss spreading across the front of his pants.

Where the hell was the boat?

Anderson stomped through the surf and swept his flashlight over the rolling dark water.

"Deputy!" Anderson yelled. "You gotta be fucking..."

First to the left and then to the right. There was only water. Dark and freezing as it relentlessly pounded the beach.

And then he saw it.

A piece of wood painted white stuck out from the waves like a broken buoy.

Anderson stomped out deeper into the ocean as he kept his light pinned to the wreckage of the *Gypsy*.

He was staring at the point of the hull. It was now pointing straight up toward the sky as if it were a rocket, ready to blast off.

The boat had sunk. He was trapped. They were all trapped.

Anderson took another step toward the sunken boat and felt the icy water lap over his groin. He shuddered, but he barely felt it. His eyes were locked on the distant lights that dotted the mainland.

Warm houses and friendly people.

No one was coming for them.

A gust of wind at his back blew him farther out a half step. His soaked boots and clothes made him feel like he was encased in concrete. Awkward and heavy in the swell of the tide, as he drifted forward, drawn to the lights across the dark water.

The tide swept past him with a hush and then rolled out again, and pulled him deeper. He wanted to go. Desperately. He was so scared and alone and he just wanted to go home.

But he needed to go back to the well. Tell the others about the boat. Maybe the wifi connection the Kaminskis had set up would save them. They could use it to call the Coast Guard. They could be rescued.

Anderson lifted his right foot, and tried to pull it out of the wet sand but he couldn't. He stared down at the dark water and yanked again. Still nothing.

"You gotta be fucking kidding me." He whispered, and reached down into the water and yanked on his legs.

Pale hands exploded out of the dark water and grabbed his wrists.

Anderson screamed and fell backwards into the water. Freezing salt water filled his mouth, and slipped down his throat and sent an electric current of shock and pain through his body.

On his back, under the crashing waves, Anderson clawed for the surface as hands tipped with black fingernails wormed their way out of the soil, and clamped onto his legs and locked him into place.

His lungs burned with the lack of oxygen. He felt a hand slide over his right kneecap and pull it toward the ocean floor with a vicious yank. A bright flash of pain exploded across his vision in a field of stars, as his knee was forced to bend the wrong way until the joint snapped.

Anderson screamed again, and let the sea to rush into

his lungs. More hands snaked up through the soil and ripped through clothes, and dug into his flesh.

Fingers hungry for bone. They hooked into his mouth and his eyes until his entire body was pinned to the rocky ocean floor.

Still, the pain rose and rose. Fingers tunnelled into Anderson's eye sockets on either side. Hands filled his mouth and burrowed into his throat. Finally, Anderson felt, more than heard, a dry crack of splitting wood as his skull collapsed and darkness swept inside.

CHAPTER

FIFTY

S arah's flashlight jerked across the stairs as she climbed the last flight. Her thighs burned but she pushed the pain away. Her daughter, her little baby, was somewhere in this crumbling building. She didn't know why, and she didn't care. She needed to find Rose and get away from this place.

The cold and the damp had settled in her bones, and she could feel it penetrating her lungs with every wheezy breath.

She dragged herself up the stairs by the banister and landed on the second floor foyer. She swept her light over the hallway choked with shadows and littered with furniture and bits of garbage.

"Rose? Where are you?" Sarah cried. "ROSE! Answer me!"

Sarah didn't wait for a response. She stomped down the filthy hall with its crumbling plaster and its floorboards softened by years of rot and water damage. She poked her light into every room she passed, probing the darkness and chasing away shadows.

Still nothing. No one.

Sarah picked up her speed. Images of her sweet little Rose falling through a hole in the floor and impaled on a piece of rebar flashed through her mind. Was Rose alone up here? Was some maniac living on the island hurting her?

Sarah's breath puffed out in ragged clouds, and she could feel her heart beating painfully against her ribs. She came to the last room and speared the darkness before the hall bent toward the east end of the building.

"ROSE!"

"Mom!"

Sarah's heart leapt and she took off toward the sound.

Around the bend the next hallway stretched into darkness. Sarah's light bounced over the walls and the floor, flashing across a silky black puddle.

"Mom!" Rose said. "Stop! The water! Please!"

Sarah's light found her daughter's face beneath the little white toque, but Sarah didn't listen. She powered through the rotten smelling water and scooped up her daughter.

Sarah squeezed her hard enough she thought she would hear her ribs creak and then set her down and checked her from head to toe.

"You're okay." She said, more to herself. "It's okay. What are you doing here, baby? How did you get here?"

Rose's face was pale and her eyes were red from crying.

"He made me come here. I had to hide in the boat. He said they would hurt you if I didn't. I'm so sorry, Mommy."

"What are you talking about? Who told you that?"

"He made me, Mommy. He made me."

"Who? Who made you come here?"

"He said if I didn't come, something terrible would happen to you and Daddy. Something really bad."

"Rose." Sarah said, "Look at me. Who told you to come here?"

Sarah held her daughter's tiny face in her hands as tears spilled down her cheeks.

"Sean." Rose whispered. "Sean told me."

Sean.

Even with everything going on. The island, the lepers, the building ready to fall around them. The mere mention of her dead son's name had the ability to leave her breathless.

"He did, Mom. I swear!" Rose told her.

Sarah nodded and grabbed Rose's hand.

"Come on, honey." She said. "It's okay."

"I'm not lying." Rose insisted. "I'm not."

Sarah led Rose back to the doorway and froze. The black, brackish water she had run across had spread and somehow grown thicker. It moved like sap, as it congealed around the doorframe.

"We can't go that way." Rose whispered.

Sarah swept her flashlight around the room. There was no other way.

"Just...come here." She told her daughter and scooped her up onto her hip. "Just hold on."

Sarah shifted her daughter into place and stared around the room behind her. She could take a bit of a head start, but by her estimation it was about six feet across to the other side of the puddle. She could have all the starting space she wanted, and she would never clear that. Especially not with a child on her hip.

And the puddle was getting wider.

Sarah shuffled back a few feet and Rose gripped her neck in a death grip, and buried her face against her shoulder.

"Just hold on, honey."

Without another thought Sarah charged forward, arms and legs pumping, and jumped through the doorway. For a moment she was sure she would clear the filthy tide.

Then her left foot splashed into the dark water and kept going. Her left leg was swallowed whole by the foul liquid, followed by her right. Her chest hit the edge of the floorboards that were untouched by the swill, and Rose was knocked out of her arms and sent tumbling down the hall.

Sarah screamed, as she felt fingers move over her legs. Desperate hands slipped over her ankles and slid between her thighs.

"Mommy!" Rose screamed and scurried back to the edge.

Sarah reached up and grabbed the edge of the doorframe, and kicked, and bucked, and pulled herself out of the muck. Greedy fingers raked across the backs of her legs and snagged on her boots.

Rose leaped forward and grabbed her mother's shoulder, and leaned back, putting every ounce of her seventy pounds into the operation.

Sarah scrambled out of the oily puddle, the bottom half of her body dripping with black residue. Fresh wounds carved into the backs of her legs stung with pain and bloomed with blood as she struggled to her feet.

Her flashlight was still spinning in the hall where she had dropped it. She scooped it up and speared the beam at the murky puddle, as bone-white hands gripped the solid edge and pulled themselves into the hall.

Sarah watched as the top of a shrouded head emerged from the centre of the puddle. Its face obscured by the filthy veil, it swivelled toward her and Rose.

Its hollow eyes bored into them. The smeared vision of its features arranged themselves into an expression of rage and ruin. Hate radiated from the figure's face that exuded corruption and pain. And others followed.

They emerged from the muck and crowded the narrow space, each one desperate to enter the hall and claim the kill for their own.

Sarah didn't look back.

FIFTY-ONE

Sarah grabbed Rose's hand and ran down the hall, her flashlight aimed in front of her, as her daughter struggled to keep up. This was not the way she had come, and she had no idea where she was going. She didn't care, as long as it was *away*. Away from the water. Away from the darkness of this place.

The hall bent again, and Sarah dragged Rose onto a central landing with a set of stairs running up and down.

"Let's go, honey." Sarah whispered, and tugged Rose along toward the stairs that led to the ground floor. Her light illuminated the risers a few at a time, until she shuddered to a stop. Oblivious to what lay ahead, Rose piled into Sarah from behind and almost knocked her mother into the gaping hole where the stairs should have been.

The stairs weren't broken or shattered. They were gone. Destroyed.

Sarah gripped the shaky banister with both hands to stop her progress and nearly dropped the flashlight.

"Back upstairs, honey." Sarah said. "Back!"

Sarah had no choice but to head upstairs. Faster and faster, she dragged Rose behind her. Together their feet pounded up the warped and rotten risers as they creaked and groaned under their weight. They stomped onto the third floor landing as lightning ripped at the sky and strobed the interior of the barracks with a flash of brilliant white light.

There was no one in the hall. Not yet. Rain slashed at the windows and hammered what remained of the roof. Streams of water trickled and flowed from the various holes in the ceiling and collected on the floor in suspicious pools.

"Mama." Rose whimpered. "The water."

"I know, baby." Sarah said, pulling Rose close. "Stay close to me."

They made their way down the hall as fast as they could, and did their best to avoid all puddles. They had to reach the stairs on the opposite side of the building. Sarah prayed they were still intact.

Darkness had fallen like a stone and crushed what had remained of the watery sunlight. No stars shone tonight and even the moon was hidden behind a fortress of storm clouds.

The hall bent and ended in a window that overlooked the rear of the building and the sea beyond. Lightning lit the sky on fire again and in the flare of light Sarah saw what awaited for her and Rose.

"What is it?" Rose asked. She stared at her mother's pale face, her complexion the colour of skim milk. Rose gripped her mother's hand and it was trembling.

"Is it Daddy?"

Lightning ripped at the sky again and Sarah could see the entire rock forest from where she stood. In that split second she saw the hundreds of shrouded figures as they shuffled toward the barracks.

"Oh my God..."

"What Mommy?"

Sarah turned to her daughter and shook her head. What could she say? What could she do?

Run.

"Come on, honey." Sarah said and pulled Rose down the stairs. Together, they flew down the flight to the second floor landing where their boots splashed through an inch of dirty water.

Sarah and Rose skidded to a stop and retreated halfway back up the stairs, their eyes pinned on what awaited them on the second floor landing.

"He won't let us leave, Mommy." Rose said.

Sarah held her flashlight out in front of her like a talisman, her only defence from the dark. Its weak beam speared the centre of the little boy's t-shirt as her hand shook, too afraid to illuminate the child's face.

Sean, her son that she had watched die. Her child whose coffin she had watched lowered into the ground, stood at the bottom of the stairs.

Sarah shook her head. It wasn't real. It didn't matter that the boy looked like Sean. It didn't matter that the boy had the same crooked smile that had always melted her heart no matter what he had done.

It wasn't real.

It wasn't real.

It was...

Sean...

"Hi Mom."

Sarah couldn't help it. Hot tears spilled down her face. She could taste the salt in her mouth. She knew it wasn't real. It couldn't be.

But there he was.

Alive and beautiful.

At that moment she didn't care if it was a trick or a hologram or a delusion created by her own broken mind. Her son was standing right there. Right in front of her.

"Baby..." she whispered.

"I missed you so much." Sean said. His father's chin quivered as his own tears fell from his denim blue eyes.

"Oh honey...I missed you too."

Rose stared at the flood of murky water as it ran down the risers from the third floor to splash against her boots. She pulled her mother's hand, but Sarah ignored her. Her mother's eyes were pinned on her brother as he edged closer to them.

"Mom." Rose said. *"Mom."*

"What is this place?" Sarah asked her dead son as he stepped on the first stair.

Sarah could almost smell him. The clean scent of his skin. The smell of the coconut shampoo he loved.

"It's home, Mom. You're home now. All of you."

"MOM!" Rose screamed and tugged on Sarah's wrist. Her mother glared at her, irritated at the interruption, but it was too late.

Sean stepped closer. His bare, dirty feet splashed in the rising water cascading over the stairs.

His pale perfect skin darkened. Pitted and cracked as rotten fruit. Black veins formed spidery networks, and burst and clotted beneath his sallow skin. Lesions and boils twisted and contorted his features, until they finally saw the truth of what brought them here.

Sarah and Rose begin to scream.

FIFTY-TWO

"Which floor was she on?" Dan asked, but Wayne wasn't listening. Dan saw the old man's lips moving with no sound coming out. It was a look he recognized. Wayne was in shock, or damn near close.

"Wayne!" Dan snapped. "Which floor!"

Wayne blinked and his eyes flicked to Dan for a moment before they bounced back to the well.

"Second, I think." Wayne said.

Dan stepped out of the harness and dropped the hard hat. He scooped up a flashlight and a two foot metal pry bar from the tool bag. The closest thing he had to a weapon.

Wayne grabbed Dan's arm, and held him where he stood. Dan stared at the lawman, whose eyes were fixed to the top of the well, as he watched the black sludge gush and bubble from beneath the steel plate.

Bony hands smashed and clanged into the metal

from underneath as skeletal fingers, sharpened into knives, scratched around the opening, desperate for a weakness.

"Dan, what is that? What's doing that?" Wayne's voice was small and childlike. His face was the colour of wet cement.

Dan just shook his head.

"We don't have time for that. Just help me find my family." Dan said. "Please. We have to leave."

Wayne nodded and struggled to pull his eyes away from the well to stare into Dan's.

"Okay." He whispered. "Okay."

He let go of Dan's arm and drew his service weapon from its holster. He squeezed the grip as tight as he could, but the gun still shook.

WAYNE POINTED Dan to a pair of doors that Bryan Kaminski had forced open earlier.

"Through there." Wayne told him.

Dan nodded and was through the gap between the door and the jamb as if it were greased. He swept his flashlight across the ruined interior festering with shadows and wet from the rain that dripped through the roof. He raced over the rotten floorboards curled up and bloated with rot as he searched for any sign of his wife and daughter.

"Sarah?" He screamed. "Rose?"

Wayne took more time getting through the jammed

doorway, but he managed, and met Dan at the bottom of the stairs.

A scratching sound rose all around them. The sound of an army of rats burrowing through the walls. Wayne looked like he might be sick as his eyes flicked to the shadows that gathered and pooled in the dark corners of the ruined building.

"Dan." Wayne said, as he searched for the source of the sound. "We can't stay here."

"Sarah! Rose!" Dan yelled again.

"Dan, we have to leave."

Dan whirled on him, his face furious with worry and rage. "I'm not leaving them. I'm gonna check the second floor. Take the far stairs and meet me in the middle."

Every creak and crack in the dark yanked Wayne's head in that direction as if it were tied to a string. Dan couldn't wait any more.

"Or go if you want to. To the boat." He said to the old man. "But don't you fuckin' leave us here."

Lightning flashed and thunder shook the crumbling structure and it seemed to snap Wayne out of his funk. He shook his head and his eyes cleared. They were focused now.

"I'm coming." He told Dan. "I'll find the stairs on the other side. Meet you on the second. Nobody's leaving nobody here. Quicker we get out of here the better and watch your goddamn step. This whole place is set to fall apart."

Dan gave the lawman a grateful nod and headed up the staircase to the left.

"Sheriff." Dan said, and forced Wayne to swing back around. "In the tunnel, at the bottom."

Wayne stepped closer to Dan.

"You asked me what I saw?"

The Sheriff nodded, as he waited.

"I saw bodies, Wayne." Dan told him. "Bones. There were people wrapped in rags…"

"Lepers? Dan, *seriously*?"

"I don't know what the hell they were." Dan said quickly. "I don't know. Call them what you want, but… but that's what I saw, and that's enough for me. I'm getting my family and getting the fuck off this island."

Wayne stared at the younger man, as he looked for the lie. The scam. But all he could see was the fear. Pure and simple.

"Let's get your family."

FIFTY-THREE

Dan stomped up two stairs before his boot pushed right through the riser. His ankle twisted sharply to the right, and he swore a blue streak as he gripped the banister for balance.

He yanked his boot out of the mess of broken wood, as splinters raked his calf. Blood seeped through his jeans, but he could still stand. *Thank God.* He thought.

"Sarah! Rose!"

His voice echoed up the creaky wooden staircase but there was still no reply. He wanted to run up the risers, but the stairs looked ten years past condemned.

"I'm coming!" He called, and began his ascent.

He took the steps as fast as he could, careful to keep his boots on the outside edge of the riser, hoping that the boards beneath were still solid.

As soon as his boots were safely planted on the second floor landing, he heard a woman's guttural scream. A knife of pure primal fear stabbed him through the chest and pinned him in place. He couldn't breathe.

Sarah.

The sound came from the third floor directly above him. When the scream came again, it ripped through the smothering silence of the barracks.

Dan kept one hand gripped on the wobbly banister as he raced up the risers to the third floor. With every step he took, the rotten stairway creaked and lurched under his weight.

Sheriff Wayne Roberts heard the scream as well, and just like Dan, he froze for a second as his heart fluttered wildly inside his chest like a frightened bird. He thought of his wife reminding him to take his *dang pills*, and the way she set them on a napkin next to his bowl of oatmeal. *Blood pressure isn't going to lower itself you know.*

The scream came again and just as ugly. A desperate, pleading scream that he recognized. It was a scream of pain and loss.

Oak Bay was small, but as the only Sheriff for the last two decades, he had done his share of death notifications. Telling the living parents of a young boy that their baby was dead. That their daughter wouldn't be coming home because she drove home drunk instead of paying the $13.50 for a taxi.

He knew that scream.

Wayne pressed his back against the soaked plasterboard and shone his light up the staircase where the sound had come from. He held his flashlight in his left and gripped his service revolver in his right. He still didn't like the way his hands shook, but he was there, and he still had a job to do.

Wayne's light flickered as he carefully made his way up the stairs, mindful to avoid the soft spots as best he could. At the second floor landing he saw that the stairs leading up to the third floor were gone. They lay in moldy splinters and twisted pieces of lumber. He shone his light up to the third floor landing and hollered, "Sarah? Rose?"

He waited but there was no response. No more screams. Wayne's heart kicked up into another gear. He wished he could hear something. Crying. Whimpering. *Anything*, but silence. Silence meant death in his business. He looked for a way to climb up but gave up on that notion almost right away. He wouldn't be any good to anyone twisted and broken on the floor if he fell. He would cut across the second floor and check the stairs on the opposite side. There had to be another way up.

Wayne stepped into the second floor hallway and stopped. Halfway down the hallway, facing away from him, was Sarah. Wayne opened his mouth to call to her, but stopped. His lungs suddenly filled with syrup.

Something was wrong.

The woman stood not thirty feet away, but something was very wrong.

He could feel an electric current in the air. Crackling.

Like the air before a storm. His boots wouldn't move and his tongue wouldn't speak.

He played his light over the woman's slender frame and saw that she stood in a puddle of dark water, and the puddle was expanding, spreading out from where she stood, as if she were the source of the black liquid.

"Sarah?" Wayne asked finally.

His voice was hoarse and weak, halfway between a whisper and a croak. The woman didn't move. Didn't speak.

Wayne stepped toward her, and his eyes scanned left and right, looking for the trap. His mind screamed at him: *Nononononononono*

Something was wrong. Dead wrong. But Wayne shook it off and slowly edged closer. He passed an empty doorway and speared the darkness with his flashlight, finding only rotting furniture and flickering shadows.

"Sarah." He said. "Look at me. I'm gonna get you out of here. Get you home."

He aimed his light at Sarah's thin back and found that she had turned to face him like he'd asked.

He was about ten feet away now, close enough to step into the puddle spreading beneath her boots. His light played over the young woman's face.

Her smooth, porcelain skin was withered and wrinkled as if she had aged a hundred years during the last time he had seen her. Her eyes were as black as the bottom of a coal mine, but he could see that something flickered and sparked deep within the darkness of her gaze. These weren't the eyes of a young woman, a mother, a wife, any longer. It was a thing. A mockery, a distortion of what was.

Her glittering, ebony eyes were those of an animal. A predator.

"But I am home." The Sarah-thing said. "We all are."

Wayne couldn't move. He couldn't even think. He could barely turn his head away from the monster standing and smiling in front of him with her tiny pointed teeth, as thunderous running footsteps sped toward him from his left.

He finally wrenched his head to the left in time to see a flicker of movement, a weighted shadow burst out of the room and slam into him.

His finger, already wrapped around the trigger of his pistol, yanked off a shot that blasted uselessly into the floor as he was lifted off his feet and carried backward.

Lightning flashed and in that brief strobe of light Wayne recognized his son, Jimmy. His skin was torn in jagged wounds that exposed rotten teeth. His boy grinned and stank like stagnant water as he held him in a ferocious grip, and forced him through a doorway and into an adjacent room and then further and further still.

"Jimmy, please! Wait!"

If he heard the words, Jimmy gave no indication. Wayne's heels dragged on the floorboards as he struggled and writhed in his son's iron grip. Wayne clawed at his son's face and tore a thick flap of skin from his cheek. He cried out and felt his bladder give way as Jimmy pushed his father away and sent him crashing through the shattered window of the second floor.

Wayne dropped like a rock through the freezing night air. His terrified scream was cut brutally short as his body stopped suddenly. Tips of the wrought iron fence that bordered the barracks punched through his chest and his spine cracked like arthritic knuckles over the metal barrier, nearly severing his body in two.

Dan charged up the stairs to the third floor as his flashlight flickered and died.

"Sarah? Rose?" He said desperately. "Talk to me. Where are you?"

He slammed his hand into the side of the flashlight, but it wasn't coming back. He swore and tossed it aside as he crept through the shadows that had flooded the third floor hallway.

"Sarah? Come on, baby. Say something. Please."

Thunder rumbled overhead and the sound of the driving rain drowned out every creak and groan of the floorboards as he edged along. Lightning flashed and illuminated a ruined hallway. Water dripped through a million weak spots in the ceiling and flooded the floorboards.

Dan arrived at the first door in the hall and peered inside. He pulled his phone and activated his flashlight and swept the weak light over the interior.

"Sarah?"

A dirty bare mattress lay wedged into the corner of the room. A dark stain had bloomed across the corner.

"Rose?"

Dan's voice had taken on a hoarse, whispered quality now. He knew silence was the enemy. If they were hurt, he had to act fast. He needed to get them out of this building. Off this island. A million miles away if he could manage it.

"Sarah? Answer me." He begged the darkness as he shuffled down the hall.

Outside, the storm moved closer, it hovered directly above them now. Thunder exploded with a dry crack and shook the weakened structure. Dan felt dizzy as the floorboards shook and wobbled beneath him. He prayed for the rotting building to hold on, just a little bit longer.

Dan's boots sloshed through puddles that deepened the further he ventured into the darkness. His heart beat a mile a minute and he could hear nothing else except the rising drumbeat in his ears.

"Rose..."

He held up his flashlight when he heard it. A noise that wasn't running water. It wasn't quite a whisper. It was something smaller. Quieter. The gentle scrape of a footstep. The wheeze of a tortured breath.

"Rose?"

He took another step deeper into the hallway, past an open doorway. Dan stepped to the doorframe, and shined his pathetic light into the room, and hoped he would find his family. And prayed that he wasn't too late.

"Daddy..."

Dan froze. His breath caught in his throat. He stood completely still. Did he hear that? Was that a voice? Or just his mind playing tricks as it took the white noise of the old building and twisted it into something he so desperately wanted to hear.

"Rose?"

He left the doorway and continued down the hall, inch by inch. Dan kept the flashlight on his phone held ahead of him, as a talisman, with a whispered prayer on his lips.

"Sarah?"

"Daddy."

That voice. He knew that voice. He had heard it and it was real. It was Rose.

Dan ran through the deepening water that had flooded the third floor hallway. He splashed through the murky depths to the last room at the end of the hall and shut out everything else. The storm. The alarm bells in his head. The dread that grew like a festering cancer in his stomach. Nothing mattered as he chased the voice of his daughter into the dark.

FIFTY-FOUR

Lightning flashed over the water and Ruth saw the island in stark contrast. *That fucking island.* She thought.

She had paced back and forth for over an hour after hearing Marcus' voice on the telephone. She left the receiver to dangle on its spiral cord. It bobbed and spun until it finally came to rest against the kitchen wall.

She stood and stared out at the vast dark water, and listened to the storm grow closer. To the wind, as it howled over the waves and shook the house. No doubt pulling shingles from the roof and knocking down tree limbs. She stood there as she decided what she would do. What could she do? She thought about calling the State police, but they would be an hour away, if at all. She was alone. She had to act.

Without really thinking it through, she grabbed her raincoat from the hook by the door and stepped out onto the front porch. Lightning tore at the onyx sky and she saw the white spray of the waves crashing against the pier. She saw Marcus' little fishing boat as it bobbed wildly in the maelstrom.

Before she could talk herself out of it, she strode down the porch and to the stone walkway. In less than a minute, her face was wet with rain and her rubber boots were stomping over the slick boards of the pier.

You're a stupid old woman. Her mind scolded her. *You're going to get yourself killed. You're too old and scared to help anyone.*

Still, Ruth stepped carefully into the fishing boat and moved to the stern and primed the engine. After goosing the engine with gas, she pulled the starter cord.

They're already dead.

The voice stopped her, and she stared back at the island in the shadows, hidden in the dark.

They're already dead, Ruth. Her mind whispered. *And you know it.*

Ruth pulled the ripcord again and again. She shook her head and if anyone was watching they would see an old woman with her jaw set. Her face determined on the task at hand: to get that engine running.

The little two stroke coughed to life and quickly cycled until it was grumbling, ready to rumble. Ruth removed the tether from the pier, duck-walked to the back of the boat and hunkered down. She twisted the throttle and she aimed the little boat out to sea. Toward the island.

Praying the voice in her head was all wrong.

DAN RUSHED to the end of the hall and waded through knee high water. Someone was whimpering. The sound was pathetic and sad. A helpless child with a skinned knee at the park. A child that was trapped and in danger. Dan powered through the water, his tiny flashlight gripped in his hand.

Rose was hurt. Probably cold and wet. He needed to get to her. And then something changed. The sound. Dan slowed as he reached the doorframe and listened.

Someone wasn't crying. He knew what crying sounded like. No. This wasn't crying.

This was laughing. Giggling. An insidious chuckle that certified the feeling that had spread through his chest and gripped his heart.

His hands shook as he aimed his phone's flashlight into the last room.

"Dan?"

Dan couldn't see into the room. It was too big and too thick with shadows. Half of him wanted to rush in, but the other half kept him pinned in place. A voice in his head screaming *NO!*

"Dan...please." Sarah begged him from the dark. "Please...it's wonderful."

Dan's hand ached as he peeled it from the doorframe.

"He's here, Dan." She whispered.

Dan edged deeper into the darkness, and his flashlight revealed the room a few inches at a time. The rippling brackish water had climbed up over his knees.

Dan knew it doesn't make sense, but he couldn't stop. He had no choice.

"He's here, Dan." Sarah repeated. Her voice was a slow drawl. She sounded almost drugged. "They all are. Everyone."

Tears streamed down Dan's face as he moved forward, automatically. He couldn't stop, even if he wanted to. And he wanted to.

His light illuminated the rippling water, and then his wife's pale, bare foot, just beneath the surface.

"Everyone is here now." Sarah said again, just above a whisper. "Everyone."

Dan's hand shook so badly he thought he might drop the flashlight but he had to see. He had to know.

Sarah was seated on the ground, her arm curled around Rose; who lay across her lap, her pale shredded face, rested half in and half out of the dirty water. Her single visible eye stared up at him. Once so blue and vibrant, now a cloudy marble. Under her other arm was their dead son, Sean.

His eyes were as dark as midnight, and fixed on his own.

"Oh my God...Sarah..."

"It's all right, Dan." She whispered. "Don't be scared. We're together again."

Dan watched as something moved beneath his wife's skin. Wriggling and bulging against her flesh. A tendril of cancer that blackened her complexion and forced a spidery network of cracks to spread across her face.

"Together." She whispered as putrid water leaked from her cracked lips. "Forever."

Dan backed away, as his mind shut down allowing his body to move on autopilot, as it desperately tried to protect him from any more nightmares. Any more pain.

As he retreated, so did his light, which piled more and more shadow over the horrific version of his family.

In the gloom, Rose slithered to her feet, her black soulless eyes matched her brother's.

"Don't leave us, Daddy."

He heard a scrabbling noise and the slosh of water as his family rose to their feet in the black tide. Skin flayed by sickness and disease. Black, hateful eyes stared directly at him. Their fingers were hooked into claws, ready to attack.

"You're home now, Dan." Sarah whispered. *"Home."*

Rose opened her mouth and a sound erupted from her throat that was closer to a roar than a scream.

Dan turned and ran.

He ran into the hallway and saw figures rising from the flooded floor. Shrouded figures wrapped in filthy rags. Blood and pus bled through their coverings as they tilted their faces in his direction.

"You promised, Dan." Sarah said, as she followed him out into the hall. "You promised me."

Dan raced through the nearest doorway and found himself in a long barren room. The dining room. With his weak light he navigated to the windows and stared down at the thirty foot drop. Too far.

Halfway down the room water was pouring through

a hole in the floor. Dan ran to the edge and looked down, his light only went so far, which left him with next to zero information about what lay below.

"Don't leave me again, Daddy."

Sean appeared on the opposite side of the hole in the floor. His crooked smile turned into a frown. His brown eyes were on the verge of tears. His bald head seemed to glow in the weak light. Dark bruises ringed his eyes. His skinny frame was draped in the green hospital gown that was always too big for him.

"Please, Daddy." He whispered. "You promised."

Dan's eyes flicked to the hole in the floor, and back to the thing that wore his son's face.

"You're not my son." He said, and jumped down into the darkness.

Dan landed hard on the floor below. His knees buckled and he dropped painfully to the floor covered in a foot of water. His face dipped below the surface for just a second and he felt fingers slip around his throat. Dan thrashed and kicked as more hands tried to grab him. Fingers pulled at his arms and grabbed his legs, but still he fought.

He kicked and writhed until he was on his knees and staring at an open window, the glass long since shattered. He struggled to his feet and crawled through the murky water as hands grabbed and clawed at him, desperate to pull him backward.

Dan reached the windowsill and pulled himself up, and shards of broken glass sliced through his palms.

"NO!" He screamed at the horde. "No!"

Screaming, he hauled himself over the window ledge headfirst, as his mind ran on pure survival mode. Hands held him back as they searched for a better grip, and yanked him away from the window.

A voice at his neck stole his breath.

"Please, Dan...*stay*." Sarah whispered into his ear, as her delicate hands slid over his chest, under his coat. He felt her nails slide into his skin, as easily as a knife and he screamed as she laughed in his ear. Loud and drunk and ecstatic. Hot blood spilled down his chest as he spun violently away, and ripped her claws out of his flesh.

He ran to the window and gripped the ruined edges.

"They're here with us now, Dan." She told him. "Always."

Dan didn't look back.

DAN LANDED on his right side in the black mud, and his breath exploded from his lungs in a wheezy gush. It felt like something had broken but he was too scared to worry, or even feel the pain. He felt the mud tremble and swirl, as more pale fingers like razor tipped grubs, clawed through the ground all around him.

Dan struggled to get to his feet, his head swam with pain and terror and his vision doubled, then tripled as he got to his feet. Black dots swam across his vision, but his body knew what to do. He put one foot in front of the other as pain lanced through his leg with every step and a fire burned in his chest. He could taste blood, but he could hear them coming, and that was enough to keep him moving.

Wet, sucking sounds followed him as the tortured creatures pulled themselves from the mud. He passed the well, as dark water spit out of the hole they had created. Shooting high into the sky like a geyser of evil. Pale hands gripped and fought the edges of the twisted metal plate, as they pulled themselves out of the dark to hunt. Dan shuffled into a loping run and headed for the stone arch as fast as his legs would take him, as a chorus of screams rose out of the darkness behind him.

FIFTY-FIVE

Ruth had definitely lost a few years off her life, as she navigated the waves of the storm and the rain in the little fishing boat, but she was here. She had brought a powerful flashlight Marcus had kept in the house during blackouts, and swept the wide beam over the beach. The spot where she knew Wayne would land the *Gypsy*. But the boat was gone.

Her light found the length of rope still tied to a skinny spear of rock, but not the *Gypsy*. Ruth turned in her seat, and shone the light over the rolling waves as rain slashed at her from all directions. It took her a bit, but she found it. A piece of wood stuck out of the waves and aimed back at the beach.

The *Gypsy* had somehow sunk, and Ruth's heart sank with the realization.

They're already dead.

Once again, she aimed the flashlight at the beach, and at the entrance to the rock forest when she heard a desperate scream. A moment later she saw someone limp into her blade of light. She pinned the figure with her beam. She watched as Dan scanned the empty beach, his expression confused.

"Dan!" She screamed. "Dan!"

Dan stared at her, and then shot a glance back toward the entrance to the rock forest. A moment later he took off, as he raced for the water.

A terrible noise rose and broke over the waves, that chilled her far worse than any rain or freezing temperature could do. The sound was of a charging army, as it rounded the corner of the stone maze and chased Dan down the beach, to where he splashed into the water.

Ruth couldn't move. She could barely breathe. Her light shook in her hands as it flickered over the crowd dressed in rags and filthy bandages, as they screamed in desperate agony for their prey like a savage hunting party.

Dan waded straight into the churning water and dove into the waves. A second later she saw him claw through the water, as he swam as hard and as fast as he could toward her little boat.

"Swim Dan! Faster!" Ruth screamed as the crowd behind him melted into the water after him. She watched them disappear into the waves and realized that they were both going to die.

THE FREEZING WATER hit Dan like a hammer. The breath in his lungs turned to ice and his sodden clothes turned to concrete as he swam. His boots felt like cinderblocks at the ends of his legs and his arms ached. He couldn't catch his breath and every time he surfaced he felt that Ruth and her little fishing boat were farther away.

He kicked again, and moved his arms, and dragged the water under him, as he clawed through the waves determined to push him back to the beach.

Back home.

"Swim Dan! Don't stop!" Ruth screamed. "Don't look back!"

Ruth watched in horror as the horde of shrouded creatures slithered through the water as if they were born in it. They torpedoed straight for Dan, as they glided effortlessly through the dark water. She watched as his exhausted face popped up above the waves as he caught a sip of breath. She caught his eyes in the beam of the flashlight. Flecks of denim, just like his father. She saw his face twist in pain. He opened his mouth to scream and then he was gone.

"No!" She screamed. "No! Dan!"

Ruth scanned the rolling waves. She raked her light back and forth across the rippling surface, as her heart slammed painfully against her ribs. Her mind counted through the seconds as they stretched out farther and farther...

Dead. Her mind hissed. *He's already dead.*

In a flurry of motion, Dan broke the surface three feet away from the boat and reached for Ruth. Blood ran from three deep grooves clawed across his face. He screamed like a hunted animal. Ruth caught him, leaned back and felt the muscles in her back pop, as she hauled the much larger man into the boat.

"Go!" He screamed, as he kept low in the shallow craft. "Go!"

Ruth scrambled back to the engine, as fingernails scratched across the hull. She twisted the throttle on the engine and the bow of the boat lifted in the water. Dan grabbed the fallen spotlight and fired the beam back toward the island. The white light played over the jagged, black rocks that rose like knife blades from the stony beach, and swept over the crowd of people that stood on the beach.

He saw them all.

Anderson, Bryan, Terry, and Jimmy. Even Wayne.

Everyone.

Dan shook uncontrollably, but he held the light as firm as he could as the boat bounced and bucked, as it fought against the tide, and cut through the waves to the mainland.

He had to see them.

He had to know.

A crooked finger of lightning ripped across the sky and Dan watched as the small crowd on the beach parted, as two people edged toward the water.

Rose held her mother's hand as they stood and stared out into the dark.

Staring.

Waiting.

The engine whined and the boat cut through wave after wave. Behind them the island was fading, hidden by the veil of rain and the rise and swell of the waves. After a while, the light wasn't strong enough. The beam faded.

Another brilliant flash of lightning, and Dan saw that the beach was empty.

FIFTY-SIX

Dan sat in warm clothes at the kitchen table, and Ruth had raised the heat until it was as warm as a greenhouse in the tiny home, but Dan was still cold. The cold had penetrated his bones and swam in his blood now, like a living thing. It was part of him.

A cup of coffee cooled in front of him as one of the last remaining Oak Bay deputies, a kid barely old enough to drink, sat across from him. The deputy's notebook was folded open, as he scratched his notes dutifully. Dan stared through the table, his mind a million miles away.

"I hate to keep going over this Mr. Avernus, but if you wouldn't mind...after the *Gypsy* capsized on your way to the island...what happened then?"

Dan didn't look like he'd heard the question. He didn't move or even look up. His eyes were focused on the corner of the room. A corner where shadows festered and a deep, numbing cold radiated outward from the empty spot.

The kid policeman looked to Ruth who stood against the kitchen cabinets, as she cradled a cup of Earl Grey tea in both hands. She met his gaze and gave him a little shrug.

"Dan?" The deputy asked.

Dan raised his head then. A small gesture, but one the deputy could work with. The cop could see that the man's eyes were ringed black. His skin was pale to the point of being translucent. Tiny red and blue veins were visible through the thin flesh of his face. His voice, when it came, was barely a whisper.

"*What?*"

"You said the boat capsized?" The deputy asked. "And...and then what?"

Dan spoke to the table, his voice barely audible.

"They were gone." Dan said. "All of them."

Dan lowered his head and returned his stare to the table.

"And you didn't see anyone else make it off the boat?"

Dan shook his head slowly.

The cop shot a look at Ruth who sipped her tea. He had already spoken to her and taken her statement. With no other questions the young man folded his notebook into his pocket and stood. The legs of his chair scraped against the tile floor.

"We still got people out there, searching." He said.

"Good people. Some locals even with their private boats, and the Coast Guard too. They won't stay lost for long."

Dan knew better. He knew they weren't lost. He knew exactly where they were.

"We'll bring them home, sir." The deputy assured him. "Mark my words." The deputy eyed the corner of the room that so entranced Dan Avernus, and saw a small dirty puddle of water had gathered there. He changed his focus to the shattered man who sat shivering under a blanket.

"Like I said, Dan." He told him. "One way or another, everyone will be home soon."

Home

EPILOGUE

Dan hadn't been eating. Food, no matter how rich, had lost its flavour and tasted like ash in his mouth. As a result, he'd lost weight. The bones of his skull looked too sharp beneath his thin skin. His clothes hung from his withered frame and when he stood up too quickly black dots swam across his vision.

Every day, Ruth followed him from room to room, her expression pinched with worry. She fixed him meals he didn't eat, and tea he didn't drink. She tried to reason with him, to nurture him, to care for him, and even threatened him. But nothing got through. He was no longer there. Not really.

He spent his days sitting in the master bedroom staring out at the island and waiting for her to come.

Every day he willed away the sun. He waited for nightfall.

He waited for the darkness to spread across the water

like spilled ink. For the shadows to pool in every crack. To fill every hollow. He stared out at the dark, rolling sea until every spark of light was smothered completely. Because it was then, and only then that he could hear her.

Her soft voice just out of reach. A whispered breath of a child.

Come home

RUTH LOOKED up from her book as Dan stomped down the stairs from the second floor. It was unusual for him to move from his room until dawn, and only then when Ruth opened the curtains and cajoled him downstairs for breakfast. But now he moved with purpose, with an urgency she hadn't seen since that fateful night.

"Dan?"

A stab of fear slid between her ribs and scraped bone as she heard his heavy boots march toward the back door.

"Is everything all right?"

The only answer she received was the back door as it slammed against the jamb.

Ruth set down her book and followed the noise to the kitchen.

"Dan?"

She saw his coat was missing from the hook. Ruth rushed to the window and saw his narrow frame as it moved down the stone path to the pier. Her breath caught in her throat. She took only a second to grab her coat as she rushed out there herself.

"Dan! Dan, wait!"

But he was too far ahead. He was too determined. Head hunched down, shoulders forward. He stepped down into the fishing boat and fired up the little engine on the first try.

Ruth's wheezing breaths smoked in the cold, night air and trailed behind her like a locomotive as she raced down onto the pier.

"Dan please." She begged. "Please, don't."

Dan untied the mooring line and found her gaze. Ruth opened her mouth to protest. To argue. To beg him to stay, but the words died on her tongue.

In the starlight his face appeared as hollowed out and as alive as a jack-o-lantern. His eye sockets were deep black wells. His skin was the color of parchment.

"Goodbye, Ruth."

Tears trailed down her cheeks as she stood in the blistering cold and watched him go. Until the little boat was nothing more than a tiny dot in the rolling tide. Until the boat dipped below the black waves and the darkness swallowed him whole.

IN THE HOSPITAL WAITING ROOM, Dan and Sarah sat on uncomfortable chairs as they waited for more results, more information, any good news about Sean's condition. It had been hours

since anyone had eaten anything and way past Rose's bedtime, but everyone, even Rose, had been brave and strong. She sat curled on Dan's lap, her head on his chest. He could still smell the coconut in her thick, black hair and the freshness of her skin.

"When can Sean come home?" Rose asked.

"I don't know, sweetheart." Dan told her, as he pulled her closer and dropped a kiss on the top of her head. "But whatever happens, we'll be together, as a family."

Rose looked up at him then. Her green eyes locked onto his, as she searched for the lie. The half-truth.

"You promise?" She asked.

"Together forever." Dan told her. "Forever."

DAN GUNNED the engine and steered the little boat straight up onto the rocky beach. Rocks and bits of gravel scraped against the hull as the craft came to a stop. He stepped out onto the shore and tied the bow line to the nearest column of rock.

He snapped on his flashlight, but he didn't need it. The path through the maze of the rock forest to the barracks had been gouged into his brain. He could have gotten there blind.

He moved at a steady pace through the blind lefts and the wide rights until he crossed beneath the stone arch and into the clearing.

As he moved closer to the ruin of the well the sound of the crashing surf grew quiet. The howling wind was reduced to a low whistle, as if the island itself was holding its breath.

Waiting.

Dan stepped to the well and heard a familiar sound. His heartbeat ratcheted up and his mouth ran dry. The scratching sound of fingernails on stone grew louder.

Dark, brackish water filled with bits of bone and flesh bubbled and poured out of the hole they had made in the capstone. The foul liquid pooled across the concrete cap and dripped down the ebony sides. Voices rose together, as they rushed out of the darkness. He heard their panting breath, and their sharpened nails as they gouged into stone, as they climbed the well to finish the hunt.

They were coming.

He heard another sound to his left. A softer sound. A child's voice. Barely a whisper. And then he felt a tiny, cold hand slip into his.

"Welcome home, Daddy."

AUTHOR'S NOTE

Lake Avernus is a volcanic crater lake in the Avernus crater in the Campania region of southern Italy. According to tradition, all birds flying over the lake would fall dead. This was likely due to the toxic fumes expelled from the mouth of the crater into the atmosphere.

In later times, the word Avernus was simply an alternative name for the underworld, as the Romans believed it to be an entrance to Hades.

Although most of the accounts in this book are fiction, it is true that from 1891 to 1924, D'Arcy Island in British Columbia, Canada, was used as a leprosy colony, where thousands of people, mostly Chinese, were quarantined and essentially left to die.

WHAT DID YOU THINK?

Hi there!

You made it to the end of **AVERNUS ISLAND** and I truly hope you enjoyed it.

If you did please take a minute to leave a short review on Amazon and Goodreads. Reviews mean the world to a indie horror author like myself and I would be eternally grateful for this small kindness.

Look for book 3 in the Monsters & Mayhem Collection: **GOD OF THE DEAD** coming soon!

THE
GOD OF
MONSTERS & MAYHEM
THE DEAD
COLLECTION

PATRICK McNULTY

ACKNOWLEDGMENTS

This book had a lot of help to get it from first draft to finished novel. I want to thank my wonderful Beta Readers, and the amazing reviewers whose continued support means more than they will ever know.

Danielle Yeager (**Hack & Slash Editing**)
Miltiades Theodossiou
Leigh Kenny
Samantha Robinette
Emily Haynes
Chandra Marie
Erika Poynter
Kylee Jones
Sammi Dyer
Kyle Rolinatis
Jenni Leonard
Liz Priest Wallace
Mallory Elliott
Andrea Cervantes
Sharon Elwell
Lorrie VanMeter
Phil Baker
Mia Dalia

Kate Sandberg
Jennifer Mitchell
Ellisa Destiny Lott
Nick Clausen
Seth Wimmer
Jordan Triplett

Thank you all so much for your diligence, your patience, your help and for being the kind of fans, and friends, a guy like me could only dream of.

ALSO BY PATRICK MCNULTY

The Ministry of Monsters Collection

A Dark Breed

Avernus Island

God of the Dead (coming soon!)

The Danny Devlin Series

Follow the Devil

Ratter Road

Blood Debt

The Ministry of the Wraith Universe

Sleepers Awake

The Blood Singer